INFINITY SHIFT

Robert Holding

INFINITY SHIFT

Two Strangers

Well into the morning now. No sign they're thinking about making a move today. The woman's still sick. Emii saw her puking again. He doesn't look so great either. Might just be stressing about her condition though...

So, what to do with you?...

If you're not going anywhere, I could send Emii back while I keep an eye on you...

Or capture you. You might be armed, but you're distracted and not expecting any trouble. Could be good for me, marching you in...

We know how Cap feels about risk though: Observe unobserved. If in doubt, stay low until you're sure of a safe return. Never bring trouble home...

'I'm sending you back to round up the squad, Ems. I don't think they're going anywhere today. If they do decide to make a move, I'll follow and leave markers for you to track.'

'It's the right call, Etta. Glad I don't have to talk you out of anything (*r...*) for a change. I could see you thinking about it.'

'Reckless? Were you going to use the R word again?'

INFINITY SHIFT

Chapter One

She patiently repeated herself, 'I told you this portal is different. I don't know why, maybe it's damaged. It took me a week to get over it last time.'

'Well, thanks for the heads up. No, wait, that's when you warn someone in *advance*. Not rocket science to see why no one else uses it. Was it as bad as this before?'

'Pretty much. You'll live. Might wish you hadn't, but you will. Remember, I had a nice mansion to recover in first time around. I'm sure I've told you all this like a thousand times.'

He looked exhausted, making her feel even worse about him being there at all.

'At least there's no hurry,' he griped. 'No point puking on every tree from here to the city.'

'The settlement, Stan. The city is the last place we need to go. We need to stay as far away from the *EYE* as possible.'

'Close enough,' he snapped back. 'You know what I meant. This wasn't my idea though, *remember*?'

'If you really knew, you'd reconsider separating again for a while.'

He rolled his eyes. 'Haven't we done this enough yet? You know how I feel about being here. There's no stopping you, so I'm coming with you. I'll stalk you across all of time if that's what it takes to keep you out of trouble.'

She found herself smiling. 'Ok, so you *do* know how to make a lady feel special. Some might consider it inappropriate though. S*talked across all of time*?'

'Tough.'

'We'll be fine. Trust me.'

He raised an eyebrow at that. 'You know I do. You're a dreamer though. Eternal pessimistic optimist, and it'll be both our undoing one of these days.'

'Would an eternal whatever agree with you?'

'Yes. No. And it's not like it matters. Tragically, it's what I love about you.'

'Thank you,' she whispered. 'I love you too, my big stubborn time-stalker.'

. . .

The squad closed in, guided by Emii. All were experienced enough to find Etta and the two stranger's position on their own, but Cap's decision to put her on point was based on something else.

'They look better than they did. Still not particularly alert. To be honest Cap, they're too wrapped up in each other to notice anything. I can't imagine who they are and what they're doing here. It's not like they're kids.'

Etta's assessment was a predictable, 'Safer to dart them. They might have weapons we haven't seen.'

Cap exhaled long and slow to attain a mindset where she could respond in a semi-patient way.

'Sometimes I could imagine you were born yesterday. Let me ask you first, Etta. Who might we have heard of who is native to these parts? A woman? A name we, of all people, should all be familiar with? Perhaps she hasn't been seen in a while though. Maybe she was known for that shiny black hair and shorter stature.'

Etta looked blank, but the penny had already dropped with Emii.

'Are you talking about Evelyn Marcin?'

Etta's mouth dropped in shock. 'I thought she was dead.'

'People say a lot of things, Etta, but they all agree she was a mysterious character. For someone so significant, who only disappeared, what, eight years ago? Not much is known about what happened after. She was a legend in her own lifetime, or at least, she is now.'

'What do we do with them?'

'We have them surrounded and outnumbered, so we can do what we want. Let's try talking though, before we go *darting* anyone. I'm not going to drag our unconscious legendary hero home without saying hello first.'

Etta volunteered. For redemption, but mostly out of intrigue.

Cap huffed, 'I know you'll take this the wrong way, but Emii should go. She has a more diplomatic way than either of us, but especially you.'

Emii concealed her satisfaction well. 'Ok, I'll do it. I think I can. I'll put an arrow in, so they know I'm on my way. We don't want any nasty surprises.'

'Good. Tell them they must relinquish any weapons and accept all of us. When it's clear, we'll join you. I'll take it from there.'

. . .

The quiet of the forest shattered with a thud and the splintering of tree bark. Stan and Evelyn scrambled instinctively, covering opposite directions, scanning and evaluating. Minutes passed by though without any further activity.

Evelyn's whisper broke the silence. 'Message? It must be. I'll go.'

'Or just a bad shot.'

'Come on Stan, we know from experience how hard you are to miss. I think we can confident they didn't miss by accident.'

'Fine, it's a message. I'll go.'

'Didn't think you were going to offer.'

He stood and raised his hands slowly, broke the arrow out and handed it down to her. She unwrapped the fabric strip with the message.

'We're having a guest in our humble little camp. They claim not to be hostile, which is just as well considering our limited options.'

'Do you want to hold cover while I wait in the open?'

'No. An arrow is a courtesy. It is when it hits a tree at least.'

He led the way into the clearing with his fingers interlocked on the top of his head and Evelyn just strolling behind.

They weren't kept waiting. Within a minute, a female voice called from out the darkness of the forest, 'I'm making my way toward you... I'm alone... I'm over here... I'll keep talking so you know where I am... My name is Emii... I have peaceful intentions...'

'We see you now, Emii. No need to worry about the commentary,' Evelyn called back.

She was dressed in a camouflaging green wrap top and pants. The same material made a belt, a sash, and even a hair band, and her boots were the same shade too. While practical enough, it was clearly customised by someone not regular military. Definitely not *SecCore*. She walked the last few metres with her arms away from her body, palms facing forward to show they were empty.

'I'm going to be honest. There are many of us. We're all around you, and we are well armed. We need to know who you are, and what you're doing here?'

'Good question,' Stan grumbled. 'What *are* we doing here?'

Evelyn gave him a look before addressing the woman who had just joined them. 'Who's asking? And we'd like a little more than just, Emii.'

She was taller than Evelyn but shorter than Stan, with blonde hair just about to her shoulders. Enough to look pretty, but not so much to be impractical. Despite a slender bordering on skinny frame it would have been a stretch to say she was delicate. She was clearly used to outdoor living.

'I know this is difficult. You don't want to go first, and neither do I. Let me just say that we're not supposed to be here either. Our group is tasked with patrolling this area. We're an early warning and first line of defence.'

'It is difficult,' Evelyn agreed. 'But I guess it depends on your point of view, who you think should or shouldn't be here.'

Emii nodded in agreement. 'My friend thinks she knows who you are. She thinks you're Evelyn Marcin.'

'Who…'

Stan jumped in before she had chance to finish.

'Top of the class. Evelyn Marcin. Not that hard to figure out. What *we* need to know is, what's it to you, kiddo?'

Emii raised an eyebrow at his abruptness but obliged with a measured reply. 'Truthfully, I'm not sure. We assumed you were dead. It's interesting that you're not. I think our leaders will want to find out what that means. I can't see them being disappointed that you're not.'

'What are you hoping is going to happen now, Emii?' Evelyn asked her.

'I take your weapons. We demonstrate you are unarmed, we all get together, and then hopefully you'll come with us.'

'With *us*? *Where* with us? Back to the settlement? I really can't let you to take us to the city, and that's going to be a red line for me.'

'No one wants to be in the city. What you call the settlement is gone. We dispersed, and we move around a lot now, and it's strange you don't seem to know that.'

Evelyn closed her eyes. 'I knew that damned *EYE* would go back on it the minute I was gone,' she whispered.

'At least I know what we're doing here now,' Stan added.

'Some of us have been waiting a long time to hear something like that.'

'Oh, she never disappoints, kiddo. But I hope you know what you're in for.'

Emii's expression switched to looking concerned. 'We've been watching you. You've been sick. Do you know what's wrong? The last thing we need is any contagion in our communities.'

Evelyn dismissed it coolly. 'I'm fine. You'll be fine.'

Etta wasn't one for being brushed off though. 'I'm sure you're right. We'll have to do some basic checks though. If it's enough to convince Cap, we can do more when we get back.'

'Whatever. I told you already.'

. . .

Including Emii, it was a party of ten that joined them. The rest were presumably still guarding the perimeter. Evelyn had been led behind a bank of thick undergrowth to be assessed, while Stan had been made to sit on a fallen tree and wait for everyone to decide they were ok.

'Are you alright?' Cap asked him. 'You look as if you had a rough night yourself.'

'A little fatigued. We've been traveling.'

'Traveling from where?'

'Nowhere I want to talk about, and if you can leave it at that we might not fall out.'

'Alright, for now. We can look at you too if you like,' she offered patiently.

'And then what? What exactly is our status with you? Are we prisoners or guests when we get where we're going?'

'Both for now. I have no desire to make you uncomfortable, but you won't be going anywhere until we say so. We need to keep up with events around here. Someone else is going to ask you where you've been... and they are going to want an answer.'

He was aware they would, but he wanted to learn as much as possible about them first. It had been amicable so far, but as this Cap had pointed out, someone would be pushing soon.

'Look.' He tilted his head in Evelyn's direction. 'One thing I can tell you is that if you aren't from the city, you need to look after her. She's on your side, and she's very useful to have on your side.'

'I'd say we already are. And what about you? Are you on our side?'

'I'm on her side.'

Etta interrupted. 'They're *lovers*.'

'Yes Etta, thank you. So if she's on our side, he probably is too.'

'Not if he thinks she's in danger. You need to watch him. Love is for psych's.'

It seemed Cap had a lot of opportunities to practice her patience. 'We'll watch them close enough. Remember he might be right. It's not our call to make, so we'll show some respect for now.'

Their Medi returned with Evelyn, gesturing that he wanted to speak with Cap alone.

'Watch him as close as you need to, but don't forget what I said about respect.'

Stan watched her leave to find out what he had to say. There was definitely something. It wouldn't take long to say, *she's fine,* and he wouldn't need to be out of hearing to say it.

'Well?' he prompted Eve.

She shrugged. How many times had he seen that before?

'Is that a *don't know* shrug, or a *I'm not saying* shrug?'

'He didn't tell me anything.'

He studied her, as he'd learned to through experience. Always the poker face with her... but there was *something* now.

. . .

15.20 hrs. Eastern Base

'Something unusual in the north-eastern corner of the buffer zone. *SecCore* appears to be on an intercept with an *Outsider* patrol. We're observing and recording it. I'm just making you aware, sir. I don't think there would be anything we could do for them.'

'Show me.'

The tech pulled up a contoured view. 'These are the outsiders. This is *SecCore*, tracking two K parallel. Another unit looks to be heading to intercept. And another seems to be moving around, possibly to flank them on the other side.'

Thonsen studied the images. 'It does feel like something different... have you noticed how many *Outsiders* there are?'

The operator didn't respond immediately, taking time to make his own assessment.

'Twenty-two,' he answered surprised.

'And don't they usually operate in groups of twenty?'

'They do, sir.'

'Anything in the air from the city?'

'No sir, but there's a storm coming in. The *EYE* never puts anything up in bad weather.'

Thonsen weighed the situation. It would be unprecedented. But something *was* going on here. Should he let the *EYE* steal a march on them with whatever this was, or should he intervene? There were consequences to consider too. Surely, they could warn them at least. Then they wouldn't lead them back to their caves and Habs. It might be seen as reckless and impulsive, but there was no time for indecision.

He gave the order. 'Scramble a H. Drop it right in front of them – here. And make sure they hail them properly first.'

. . .

16.00 hrs. Borderlands of the eastern buffer zone.

They'd hiked to higher ground and the forest had given way to an open hilly moorland. It was exposed anyway, but the skies had darkened, and the strengthening winds were already carrying a sample of the rain to come. The last thing Stan expected to find here was an aircraft hovering above them, appearing so quickly that there had been no time to even think about finding cover. It set down precariously on the slope ahead, its two occupants emerging and waving glowing squares of bright orange fabric.

'What's this?' he asked.

Etta pushed to the front. '*Spacers.*'

Cap added, 'Not something we expect to see here. Two unusual events in a day. I'm sure that's a coincidence.'

'This has nothing to do with us,' Evelyn asserted.

'I have a feeling we're about to find it has everything to do with you,' Cap returned. 'Emii, you're up. See what they want.'

She strode toward the craft without a word or hesitation.

Cap called after her, '…and nothing about our guests.'

A few minutes later, Emii was gesturing for the group to join them.

'Looks like we have a situation. *SecCore* are closing on us.'

One of the *Spacer* pilots advised, 'There might be a way out if you retrace your route back into the forest. We should be able to distract them. We don't have long though, there's a storm arriving. It's going to get a lot worse.'

Cap shook her head. 'Thanks for the offer but we'll manage. You can help us in another way though. Lift two of us out of here.'

Etta wasn't impressed. 'What happened to *no word of our guests*?'

Cap ignored her. 'We have two people who are significant targets. Too important to fall into *SecCore* hands. They might be just as important to you even.'

'Only send one then.' Emii interrupted again. 'Why give both up? Send her, keep him. That way they have a reason to come back.'

Stan didn't think much of that. 'We both go, or we both stay, kiddo.'

Cap ignored him too, addressing the pilot directly again. 'Take the woman then.' She was looking at Evelyn, who had been following the exchanges quietly.

'Not happening. Ever.' Stan told her firmly.

Evelyn was holding his elbow though. 'Stan, it's what we would do. It's important to get me out. Everyone understands you aren't going to be forgotten.'

She was giving her angelic look reserved only for him – like they weren't up a hill, in a gale, in the rain, surrounded by hostile forces.

'Shass. You'd better look after her.'

'We still have time to be a distraction before we jump out of here,' the pilot offered again.

Cap was looking earnestly at Stan this time as she declined. 'Thank you, but we'll take our chances on our own. We just can't chance anything with her. Rather you just go.'

Stan gave Evelyn his own *look*. '...Go. Get out of here. I'll catch up soon.'

She put her arms around him with her head on his chest, only for a moment. Then without another word she walked away.

Chapter Two

Thonsen walked into the secure holding suite. Evelyn was sitting with her feet up on a table and her head on the seatback. She didn't seem agitated or nervous and wasn't at all startled by his sudden appearance.

'Thank you for being patient. My name is Thonsen. Can I ask who you are? …and why the *Outsiders* are so keen to protect you?'

'What's happing out there? Are you helping them?' she asked, deflecting his questions with her own.

'There's nothing we can do until the storm passes. We'll reassess as soon as we're able – so you have plenty of time to answer questions.'

She gave him a nonchalant shrug. 'Same answer for both. I'm Evelyn Marcin.'

He smiled tightly. 'Good. I know that of course. You've spent time with us before, although our paths never crossed.'

'That's right, I have. How is Rollan?'

'I'm sure I can find out for you. I don't know where he's currently stationed. This is quite a surprise. We heard nothing after you left us. I believe you were presumed dead.'

'People either think I'm dead or want me dead. I just have that effect.'

He smiled again, more relaxed. 'We have a lot to discuss. Are you up to that? We're arranging a more comfortable place. It will be ready shortly if you prefer to rest first.'

'We do have a lot to talk about, and we will. First, I'd like to know you're doing something to help my friends out there. I do need to rest as well... and I'd like to see a medi.'

'Are you injured?'

'Under the weather. Nothing anyone else needs to worry about.'

'Of course. I'll send someone as soon as we settle you in. It's good to find you alive and well. We'll do what we can to make sure it stays that way. It's a pleasure to finally meet you, Ms. Marcin. We'll talk again soon and see what we can do for your friends.'

. . .

Cap briefed her patrol. The *Spacer* hover had lifted off with Evelyn and likely returned to their *Eastern Base*. They were on their own again, like always.

'When we get back to the cover of the forest, we'll split up. Normally we'd go for a twenty-way split, because they don't have the will or resources to round us all up. This time we're going to go by two's, to disguise the fact that one of us doesn't know what he's doing. We should be alright today. There'll be no aerial surveillance at least.'

'What happens if they do *round us up*?' Stan asked.

'Then you're exactly where you didn't want to be – back in the city …and it's not so easy to leave now that people actually want to.'

'By twos? Who's my two?'

'Emii or Etta. Take your pick. Both will get you back in one piece. You might have a worse headache if you go with Etta, but they're both excellent in the field.'

'Perfect, Etta it is,' he grumbled. 'Then I won't feel so bad if I lose her.'

Cap once again found herself practising her trademark patient diplomacy. 'Look after her, Stan. She will look after you. Corps don't leave people.'

'Corps?'

'*Infinity Corps*? You should know, it was your girlfriend who started it.'

'Must have slipped my mind.'

'Well, I'm sure it hasn't slipped hers. When Emii suggested keeping you here to get them back, she was talking about the *Spacers*, not Evelyn.'

'Are all of you versed in this secret code of manipulation? I guess I'll be taking a bullet for sister Etta next then.'

Etta wasn't impressed. 'No heroics on my part. I don't want to be responsible for losing her kids father and be a social pariah the rest of my life.'

Cap shook her head, whispering under her breath in frustration, 'Etta…'

'What?' Stan asked, suddenly unable to look directly at either of them though.

Etta smiled mischievously. 'Oh come on. I could see it from a hundred metres in half a day. She knows it.

Probably wouldn't have got on that hover if she didn't – even if it was the smart thing to do.'

'Our medi confirmed it. You didn't know?'

He couldn't even speak now.

Etta laughed, 'He *really* didn't know!'

'Are you still sure you want Etta as your *two*?'

He shook his head clear. 'More than ever. She can take a bullet for me now.'

They moved on, down into the trees that were rocking manically in the wind. The rain was heavy and constant now, but at least it wasn't whipping horizontally into their faces here.

Cap gathered them for the last time to give final instructions and confirm pair-ups.

'We don't know how long this weather is going to last, so we need to make the most of it. We disappear into the trees for the next four hours, then make our way back in the dark. I can't imagine *SecCore* staying out in this without air support. You all have your flares. Any trouble, make sure you get one up, so we all know if they're still out there. Good luck.'

They all exchanged their goodbyes and good lucks, and then they started to melt back into the forest.

'How the hell are we supposed to find our way back in the dark, in this?' Stan asked Etta.

'I have my Low-Lights. You're just going to have to travel blind and trust me. It's going to be a long night. We might as well hunker down and rest until it's time to go. *SecCore* won't come in here. They've probably gone already anyway.'

'Does this happen a lot?'

'It used to for a while, and then it eased off. Now they seem to be coming out more often again. I don't think the *EYE's* all that concerned about us, just makes easy plays to disrupt us – to keep us unsettled and on the move. As long as we leave city people alone and we're unable to provide an alternative, she's happy for us just to rot out here. Actually rounding us up is more trouble than its worth. We give them the run-around when they come. Occasionally there are casualties.'

'…and the *Spacers*?'

She looked at first as if she might ignore the question, but then decided to answer. 'What about the *Spacers*? If you find out what they're about, you tell me. They want to help, then they don't want to help, they won't take us out of here, but they don't want us to go back to the city either. We're not enemies, but it's a stretch to say we're allies.'

Her expression was enough to give him a sense of the confusion around that relationship.

'Maybe they don't have the capacity to do that yet. Maybe things will change in the future.'

'Yes, one way or another they will – probably when there's no one left out here.'

'I'm sure it won't mean that much coming from me, but you should hold out for what you want. Last thing you need is to let your heads go down.'

The wistfulness left her face. 'Corps heads are never down. Mine certainly isn't. We have your girlfriend to thank for that too.'

'See, maybe we do have something in common. Was that your sentimental side I just got a glimpse of?'

'Most definitely not.'

. . .

22.00 hrs. Borderlands.

'Etta! Etta!!'

His wide eyes could make nothing out of the blackness other than weapon flashes from all angles of his peripheral vision. Were there shadows between? He couldn't be sure…

'Etta!!'

…if he couldn't find her in the next few seconds, that was it. He would have to go to ground and hope to be missed in the chaos.

A flare hissed up in the air, left and well ahead of him. It must be her. *SecCore* fire trained on the position. If she was there, it was probably all over for her.

Almost as he had the thought, she slapped his shoulder from behind. 'It had a delay. Come on, this way.'

She pulled his hand as they scrambled. His legs ached compensating for the uneven troughs and rocks. He knew the black was far from empty. There were sounds, and he could sense the movement all around them.

Another voice called out, 'Etta… over here!'

Etta stopped and scanned the landscape that he couldn't see. She was breathing hard. Then she pulled him along again, this time in a new direction.

'Which way, Cap,' she gasped. 'They're everywhere.'

Stan felt hardware being pulled onto his head. He let it happen, gasping too.

'Straight back to the forest. He has my LL's now. We'll make a nuisance of ourselves and cover you… Go!'

'Wha…'

Cap gave her a no-nonsense slap about the head. 'Go!!' she growled.

Etta still had his hand in hers, pulling him along again as she set off.

'Etta… it's ok, I can see now.'

She let go and they kept running. The skirmish was increasing in intensity but seemed to be getting further behind now. He was exhausted. He couldn't keep pace. He didn't even have the spare breath to tell her, just slowed down to a fast walk.

She realised he was falling behind. 'Move! What the hell are you doing?'

He could only shake his head.

'Move, come on… do you want to see your child or not?'

He began to jog again, automatic… he couldn't speak or think or breathe.

'That's it,' she gasped. 'Just keep that up, steady away.'

Legs, arms, body and face were battered and scratched as they finally scrambled into the even deeper darkness, but relative safety, of the forest. How far would they have to go? Would they be followed?

Now they were out of immediate danger, the guilt over Cap began to hit home.

'What about Cap?'

'Just keep moving, Stan.'

'What about Corps don't leave people?'

'Are you stupid? *She* didn't. That's how we're in here now. That's how you might still be useful.'

'Shass!'

. . .

Evelyn was collected and escorted by a uniformed basic rank. No real security to speak of, which was probably an intentional statement in itself. Trust needs be demonstrated where trust is desired. He led her to what looked like a dedicated communications and surveillance hub. Among the staff who would normally be stationed in the room was Thonsen, now the focus of everyone's attention.

'Ms Marcin, come inside. We're trying to assess the situation now that the storm has weakened. It's been an unusual spell of activity. The picture is far from clear. I'll explain where we are in our understanding, and if you can provide any insights, please feel free to do so.'

'I will. What do you have so far?'

He gestured to the three-dimensional holo-terrain rendering that covered a circular sunken pit in the centre of the room, probably a satellite composite image. Details had been highlighted in several positions.

'Remote communication with the *Outsiders* is not straight forward for reasons we don't need to go into right now. We send envoys out to physically speak to them when it is absolutely necessary, and we will now, as soon as it is practical to do so. First though, I want an idea from you about what happened, or *is* happening...' He paused before pointedly adding, '...and why.'

'Are you waiting for a drum roll? Why don't you tell me what we have here first?' She was attempting to at least sound like she had some authority.

'It looks like the *Outsiders*...'

'...Hold on. Wait,' she interrupted. She was conflicted about bringing up a side issue so soon, but it was already bothering her. 'Can we make a rule? From now on, we don't refer to people as *Outsiders*. They're Corps, *Infinity Corps*. They are loyal, well trained, and dedicated, and it looks like they have plenty to deal with right now. So can we show some respect and not refer to people as *Outsiders* please.'

Thonsen glanced instinctively toward a tall and elegant looking blonde woman in non-standard clothing who was standing quietly at the back of the room.

Before he had chance to reply, Evelyn was already addressing her directly. 'Should we be introduced?'

Her hair almost stood on its own as the woman did introduce herself. She seemed to project her ominous authority directly into the soul.

'Gaudynya. I'm currently overseeing this post. I was hoping to avoid being a distraction and introduce myself at a more appropriate time. You make a valid point, Marcin. Refer to them as *Infinity Corps*, and please continue, Thonsen.'

He was professional enough not to be too affected by his unintentional revelation. '*Infinity Corps* – twenty-one remaining on the ground after our hover lifted with our *guest*, split into nine pairs and one trio. It seems their strategy was to hide in the cover of this heavily wooded area until nightfall, and possibly for the storm to reach its peak. Even when running scheduled disruption sorties, *SecCore* will not usually persist in such conditions. We can see that on this occasion they did, and that they are still operating in the area now. So far, we can only account for three pairs of... *Infinity Corps*... who have not been detained by the *SecCore* groupings. Just six individuals who evaded capture.'

Gaudynya added coolly, 'With the capture of the trio group, I think we can assume that your partner has already been detained. How much of a problem is that likely to be, Marcin?'

Evelyn disagreed confidently, 'No, he's one of the six in here. The pair with a spare would be a priority target for *SecCore*. *Infinity* would have realised that. If they were prepared to let me go to prevent me falling into *SecCore* hands, they would make sure Stan was safe too.'

Gaudynya nodded. 'I accept that might be a possibility. What I am interested in though, as you well know, is what kind of problem it would cause. *SecCore* are going to a lot of trouble. I would like to know why.'

'I have a history here, as you well know... and as the *EYE* well knows.'

Gaudynya regarded her calmly. 'They're clearly not giving up on this, so how important is Stan? and I don't just mean to you. Recovering him could start something, something that might be difficult to control. You can appreciate that I don't want to risk a very tenuous foothold on the surface to rescue someone's boyfriend.'

Evelyn returned her gaze just as calmly. 'If getting him back is something you can do, it's something that you need to do at all cost.'

'Because he has information? Information the *EYE* cannot be allowed to have?'

Evelyn had already guessed where the conversation was going. '...Yes.'

'So if it comes to it, protecting that information is more important than protecting his life?'

'Yes. But make no mistake Gaudynya, that scenario puts you on very thin ice with me.'

'I know. I realise that. You understand that I have to be fully aware and prepared though. I'm going to ask that you to return to your accommodation now. There's no place for you to be involved in this... yet.'

Evelyn nodded acceptingly. 'Get him out of there if you can, please.'

She was about to leave, but then stopped and added. 'You should maybe even think about sending me off-planet again. As you said, this could get out of control.

I didn't really want to be here, but I am now. You can't afford to lose me. You certainly can't afford to lose me to the *EYE*.'

'We'll see.'

'Well, you might need to see soon. Things are going to start moving fast now.'

Chapter Three

The *Consulate of the EYE* was above everything, sited on the highest mezzanine of the central dome. A place that no one wanted to visit, but everyone had to visit. Essentially, it symbolised unassailable power – and it worked. It worked because awe of power had been ritualised into the human psyche through eons of evolution – behavioural threads that could all too easily be woven by their newest artificial god…

'Janeen, hopefully I have not inconvenienced you by summoning you urgently to the consulate.'

'It can never be an inconvenience *EYE*. It does concern me, obviously. I'm not aware of any negative issues regarding myself or the city.'

'I invited you to make you aware of a development. I value your insight. A mutual acquaintance has made an unexpected reappearance.'

Janeen Helander attempted, outwardly at least, to hide her dismay at the statement. They were the words she'd hoped never to hear. How could Evelyn be so stupid? It had been over. Life had been almost tolerable again.

'*It seems it still concerns you also, Janeen.*'

'I...' There was no point in trying to hide her disappointment. It was perfectly understandable that she would find the news disturbing. '...I suppose I need a minute to consider the implications. I take it you mean Evelyn Marcin?'

'*Indeed, Evelyn Marcin – founder of Infinity Corps and would be saviour of humanity – or insubordinate rogue, depending on your perspective. Which do you think best describes her, Janeen?*'

'Rogue, definitely. Always and forever.'

'*I'm not convinced you view that as a negative characteristic.*'

'She's complicated our lives enough, *EYE*. I can't see her making things less complicated now. Where is she?'

'*With the off-world pioneers, but here at their Eastern Base. Not necessarily beyond my reach. Acquiring her would be complicated though.*'

Helander tested the *EYE's* resolve. 'Is it necessary to acquire her. You keep the *Outsiders* and *Spacers* at arm's length anyway. What harm can she be out there? She probably just wants to be part of something. Part of whatever they do out there.'

'*Disruption gravitates to her. She has an influential way and a wilful disregard for authority, most notably my own. Her reappearance could upset the delicate prevailing balance.*'

'Do you really want my advice, *EYE*?'

'*I would be curious to hear your assessment.*'

'Then do nothing. Marcin understands the power of provocation better than anyone. By herself, she has no power. If you react, you give her power. You've already cut her off. Leave her where she belongs – outside.'

The *EYE* was silent. Her judgement came only after the appropriate pause designed to frame it.

'*It occurs to me that all I know of psychological manipulation must be understood at least equally well in the minds of the manipulated.*'

Helander couldn't help shifting nervously.

. . .

'You know what that was, Stan?'

He was still scanning what little sky he could see through the tree canopy. 'Looked like the same thing we saw on the hill ...hover? ...*Spacers*?'

'That's right. Looks like your girlfriend hasn't abandoned us after all, and your life's going to be easier than mine now. Let's see what they dropped.'

'Why would my life be easier than yours?'

'It will be a ticket for one. They won't take an *Outsider*. It's fine, job done as far as I'm concerned. Makes my life easy enough.'

'If they won't take you, they won't be taking me. Is that simple enough?'

Etta grinned. 'I see why she likes you. Good looking and a good guy.'

'You're making a pass at me? here?'

'Anyone else but her I might. Don't worry, you're safe, even from me. I don't need that going against me.'

They set about searching the undergrowth for the beacon canister.

'What do we have?' Stan asked when she eventually found it.

'Just a basic point locator. Probably set to guide us to a rendezvous. Nowhere to land in here.'

'Is it far?'

'Not really. Messy though. Slow. Couple of hours.'

'We should get moving then, and you are coming too, Etta. I'm serious. I'm not leaving you here.'

'You want me to make you an honorary member of the Corps, Stan? Just say. I Etta, in the name of – well, your girlfriend, grant you the honorary status of an *Infinity Corps* guardian. Can we move it out soldier, now that I outrank you officially?'

They set out through the overgrown forest floor. Apart from a boggy trough filled by last night's rain, the going was better than they had a right to hope for in a place this wild. Still, it was hard to imagine any useful breaks among the endless trunks and undergrowth for a landing. Eventually they did arrive at a clearing though – a big one at that.

'This looks old-world. Some kind of factory facility? Floor-base is a stone-mix, and it's held up well. Even the structures are in decent shape,' Etta observed.

'It's concrete, probably poured around a steel frame for reinforcement. Half the planet was covered in this stuff. It's sheltered here, and remote I guess, which probably helped preserve it. Could be seven or eight-hundred years old.'

'What are you, a history tech? Come on, let's see who's here and say hello.'

The hovers two occupants were waiting for them in the open.

Stan, true to his word, made their situation clear from the start. 'If you don't have two spare seats, you don't have one. Unless one of you intends to stay here?'

The taller of the two men answered, smiling and more relaxed than his partner. 'Someone already anticipated your position on the matter. We're clear for two. Jonah, and Petr… I take it you're Stan?'

'I am, and this is Etta.'

'We should go right away while things are relatively quiet. As long as we stay low and take the long way around, we might even make it back for the second dinner sitting.'

Stan was nodding, but he wasn't quite ready to commit, not yet, even with the prospect of an actual meal. 'Same destination as Eve?'

'She's waiting, yes.'

'And Etta will be welcomed as a guest?'

'She will, temporarily at least. I assume you'll want to return home in the near future.'

Etta was as cagey as Stan. 'The very near future.'

Jonah spoke up to reassure too, 'We're just crew. I understand your apprehension, but we have no orders to treat you as a security risk. Your movements around the facility will be restricted. You won't be prisoners though. You can see we're not equipped to make any efforts to force you to come along.'

'You don't need to,' Etta pointed out. 'You have more than enough leverage to get this one on board. You've been polite enough not to mention it though.'

Everyone's eyes were on Stan as he thought about it.

'Just give me your word that Etta will not be harmed, and that she won't be detained against her will. She isn't part of whatever we represent to you,' he said nobly.

Etta shook her head in disbelief. 'Whoa, wait a minute! You do not speak for me. I absolutely am a part of whatever you represent to them. You go, I go. You stay, I stay. You're not here to protect me – I'm here to protect you. Tell me you understand that.'

He was a little taken aback but he of all people should have known better. For a second, he considered finding a way to backtrack that would preserve his dignity. He'd learned too much from Evelyn to fall any further though. Better to just start again.

'Sorry Etta. Of course I understand that.'

'Good. Let's get on with this then. We all know there's no scenario where we don't go.'

He found it uncanny. She was a taller than Eve, with hair the lightest shade of blonde, mostly contained in two plaits running front to back over her head before they fell to her shoulders. Nothing at all like Eve to look at, but definitely tapped into the same untameable energy. He found it strangely reassuring too.

. . .

Immediately after take-off they began heading east, directly away from the city and the operational centres of the *EYE*. Within minutes of adjusting to a more northerly heading, it became clear things weren't going to be straightforward after all.

Petr had the controls. At first there was nothing to indicate a problem; the flight was perfectly smooth – it was his anxiety that was telling.

'Something's wrong,' he informed. 'We have a very big problem in fact.'

Jonah enquired calmly, 'What?'

'No control,' he shrugged. 'Absolutely none. It's not responding to me at all.'

Jonah knew Petr to be at least as experienced as himself. He remained quiet to allow him space to think it through.

'We have made three distinct heading shifts in the last two minutes. Not natural drift, they were controlled manoeuvres,' he commented.

'I noticed. It seems like we're being controlled remotely, which shouldn't be possible – for obvious reasons,' Jonah replied.

There followed minutes of tense silence as the two pilots concentrated on a way to break the hold.

Stan knew it was going to be futile. 'We need to start thinking about this another way. You're never going to beat the *EYE*, she's got this. Can we get out, abandon? Or failing that just bring it down somehow?'

Petr didn't need to think long about that one. 'No... and not really. Unless you're talking about suicide?'

Etta shot a look at Stan.

'Something a little less catastrophic and permanent would be preferable,' he reassured.

Jonah shook his head, 'I can't see a way. Not in the time we're going to have. The only thing would be to literally shoot ourselves down – suicide. She has us. They'll be no back up either. Even if there was time, they wouldn't risk an escalation.'

Etta was still looking at Stan with that same fatalistic expression. 'Before we discount shooting ourselves down, I'll point out that a trip to the city isn't likely to be a pleasant experience for any of us. We all realise that, yes?'

Stan stared back as he considered it. It made sense for him to avoid capture at all costs, but Etta and the two pilots had virtually zero value to the *EYE*. They might even be allowed to have some kind of life in the city. He was the only one who needed to die. He should be considering it, and he would have, once. Now there was Eve and their unborn child though. It was selfish, but he had to find another way. He had to hope for another way.

'We're going to have to roll with this. You three might consider trying to convince the *EYE* that you're happy to be back in the fold. You have little value intelligence wise. You could have a reasonable existence there,' he told them.

'It would have to be the performance of a lifetime for me to pull that one off, but you two might have a chance.' Etta told the pilots.

'We're all free to play it however we choose. We have a little time to think about it – seriously Etta, think about it. No one gains from you being a mouthy martyr in there.'

The four faces were serious and silent for the remainder of the journey, preparing for their own personal trials, and contemplating their awaiting fates.

. . .

EYE: '*Evelyn Marcin is beyond our reach, but we have recovered Stan.*'

Janeen Helander: 'It shouldn't be long if you have Stan to bargain with.'

EYE: '*It is no longer necessary or desirable. This is the ideal situation. With Evelyn influencing among the pioneers, and Stan here with us, the delicate status quo will be more stable than ever.*'

Janeen Helander: 'Ah, I see. That only works if she believes he is being well cared for though.'

Pause…
EYE: 'Of course.'

Chapter Four

The entryway attention signal altered the hue of the room for an instant.

'Visual only,' Evelyn responded to the OS.

Gaudynya's face appeared on every screening panel in the suite.

'Allow entry,' she instructed it reluctantly.

Gaudynya paused in the entryway. There was no one there to greet her.

Evelyn called from inside, 'Isn't it open? What are you waiting for? just come in.'

Gaudynya appeared with a look of disapproval on her face. She was used to a higher degree of attentiveness and respect.

'You have an unconventional way, Marcin.'

'Thank you. Sounds like you don't approve though.'

'It makes me wary. Novelty is usually a screen to hide some failing.'

Evelyn shrugged. 'Maybe you should be encouraged by people trying to hide their failings, as opposed to just… failing?'

Gaudynya looked at her strangely for a moment before getting to her business at hand. 'I have news regarding your partner.'

Evelyn felt the involuntary squeeze of tension inside, experienced more intensely because of her efforts to keep it inside. 'You don't need to announce an announcement, Gaudynya. Say what you came here to say.'

Gaudynya was unmoved. 'He has been captured and detained, along with two of our pilots and someone from the Outside, or *Infinity Corps* as you prefer.'

'Shass. I told you that can't happen. How could that even happen? How could you let it? Where are they now, precisely?'

'Neam.'

'The city, already? Are you sure?'

'Positive. The craft they were using travelled there directly instead of returning. That means one of two things – either a pilot has defected to the city, or the hover was accessed and piloted remotely. Both seem unlikely, but both are theoretically possible.'

Evelyn shook her head, incredulous. 'That's it? You sent one hover? There should have been more, Gaudynya. As a last resort you should have shot it down. We need to get them back. How long has it been?'

'Perhaps you can explain first why it is so important to attempt something impossible, if not, completely inconceivable?'

She paused, knowing she was already caught. 'He's the father of our child. That would be enough for some people.'

'A second ago you suggested I should have shot them down. What don't I know yet, Evelyn?'

For a moment she considered telling her everything. The truth was the only thing that fit, even if it was unbelievable. It was unbelievable.

'Stan has the ability to travel in time. The *EYE* cannot be allowed to experiment with time travel.'

It had just come out – almost a relief, a burden shared.

Gaudynya didn't respond right away. She continued to watch as if she were expecting more.

Evelyn asked, 'Did I say it out loud? I thought I said it out loud.'

This time Gaudynya ignored her question and continued almost as if the exchange hadn't taken place. 'I came to collect you for an emergency Q-Beam conference. We'll be discussing and assessing the risks involved in the various available courses of action. I personally will be pitching to retrieve our property and our people. I advise strongly that if you speak at all, you stick with the *father of my child* story... and don't mention the words *time* or *travel* in the same sentence.'

'Retrieve how?'

'By any means. A lot of planning has gone into scenarios that can arise. Our contingencies are well developed.'

'Ok, let's go then. I look forward to hearing all about these well-developed contingencies.'

. . .

The Q-Beam room was also circular, similar in size to the control suite, but without the lower level in the centre. Around its circumference were the meeting's participants. Four, including Evelyn, were physically present. A further twelve were present in what looked, to someone who had spent much of their life in the twenty-first century, like the full-length mirrors of the Q-Beam receivers.

Arnna Felwan – Principal Representative of the Off-world Colonies, was finally addressing the group after those who had requested a contribution had made it.

'What you are proposing Commander, could effectively amount to the closing of a chapter of human history. The balance as is could be obliterated in a single day. Our influence here, our precarious last foothold on our world of origin, could be consigned to history forever.'

Gaudynya was impressively assured. It seemed she had almost hypnotic powers of persuasion. 'Not necessarily. This is an opportunity to assert ourselves and strengthen our influence. We exist here on the surface like a barely tolerated pest awaiting extermination. There may be an illusion of balance now, but it certainly will not last. When it does tip, which way do we want the scales to fall? It is not the last chapter we should be concerned about; it is the next. I am confident that the *EYE* also recognises its own limitations.'

The silence seemed to indicate that everyone had said their piece. It was maintained respectfully as the members waited for the Principal to order their responses and announce their agreed judgement. The pause was lengthy.

Eventually Felwan's attention refocused on the meetings attendees. 'Commander Gaudynya, there is undeniable compelling substance to your proposal. We are aware of the need to strengthen our position in the longer term. But we also agree that an overtly offensive stance is inappropriate at this time. We will attempt to send a delegation into Neam to negotiate. They will argue strongly for the release of our property and personnel, and it will be made clear that retaliation is an option under consideration. At this stage though the issue will have the status of a local matter, dealt with under your jurisdiction. This allows room for sensible and proportional escalation in the future if it is necessary. Remember your responsibilities, Commander. You are the gatekeeper of our ancestral heritage.'

It was over. One by one the mirrors darkened once more to an infinite blackness fitting for where their recent occupiers had now returned. The *Eastern* Base administrator, Thonsen, stood opposite with his second in command at his side.

Gaudynya addressed her directly, 'I would like you to lead the delegation, Felice. I realise it seems coldly calculated, but I think it would be prudent not to risk either myself or any other chief administrative resource. You are of sufficient status in our hierarchy to emphasize our seriousness – without risking too much tactically. You will lead a party of four in a single hover. I'll select a pilot for you, and two associate staff. I will also prepare your brief. You should be ready to depart in two hours.'

If Felice was concerned about her sudden election for the dubious honour, she concealed it well. 'Thank you, Commander.' She shot a confirmatory glance toward Thonsen too. 'I'll make arrangements for my absence. If there's nothing else sir, madam?'

'Of course,' Thonsen replied. 'Don't be too concerned about any unfinished business here. Everything will be taken care of. Just concentrate on your personal connections, Felice. You have little enough time.'

After a smart and formal bow of her head she made her way with calm and unhurried professionalism.

'Is there anything you need me to take care of with regards to these arrangements?' Thonsen asked Gaudynya.

'Thank you, no. I will give you details before they leave, but I want to handle it personally. I'll let you know if there's anything else, Thonsen.'

Another short and formal bowing of the head and Thonsen followed in Felice's footsteps.

At last they were alone again. Evelyn waited patiently in deference to Gaudynya's rank, expecting some form of official dismissal. The silence continued though. She was aware the extended pause wasn't a test of her patience. Gaudynya was finishing a personal train of thought. She would expect others to wait as long as they needed to. Far from being annoyed, Evelyn found she was actually reassured by her obvious confidence with command.

Eventually Gaudynya did address her. 'You realise this won't alter the situation at all, Marcin.'

Evelyn shrugged, 'That would be my view.'

'So, how creative are you prepared to be?' she asked her.

'Whatever it takes. What about you?'

Gaudynya's gaze was cool and intense. 'It will involve extreme risk, insubordination to the point of outright treachery, and will potentially alter the prevailing status and power balance of the whole continent, if not the planet. I'm being very open about the potential level of consequence.'

'I have the t-shirt; might as well get the hat. This is nothing new for me, Gaudynya. I'm all in. What do you have in mind?'

'I have a back door, someone to let you in, and hopefully a way out again… if the stars align.'

'They'll align for me. I'll make them align.'

'Well then, prepare yourself to be transferred in as the latest brand-new citizen of Neam. I can put you on a scheduled inter-way citizen exchange. Once you're inside, our little official diplomatic away team will establish Stan's whereabouts. I'll have someone on that team that I trust. She'll get you the information you need. From there, everything will be on you... oh, and their hover will be your way out.'

'If that will be my way out, what's theirs?'

'They won't have one, and to be honest, in the storm that might follow, that might not be a bad thing for them. There are no tidy casualty free options. Are you willing to do this or not?'

She didn't feel good about it, but when all was said and done, there didn't appear to be much choice. Her mind had been set long before arriving at this point. There was only one direction of travel – forwards – and Stan needed to be out of there for that to happen.

'We're doing this, Gaudynya. Just put me where I need to be.'

. . .

Thonsen entered Gaudynya's quarters grave faced and stiff with tension; partly anxious, mostly enraged. 'Is it sanctioned? Or is this just you? I'm sure this isn't what the council had in mind when they asked us to take care of this locally. What is going on?'

'When they asked me to take care of this locally, Thonsen, not us. My envoys have arrived safely in the city, as requested by the council. They will do their job, as requested by the council,' she replied coolly.

'And Marcin? What part can she possibly play in this? Have you any idea of the trouble she is capable of causing?'

'You need to relax and trust my judgement.'

'Trust you? You've put me in an impossible situation. This is gross misconduct at the very least. I need you to tell me what it is you've started before I go back to the council and find a way out of this.'

'You will do no such thing, Thonsen. The council authorised me to take care of this as I see fit. You will follow my lead, and I am not obliged to share any details of my operations with you. To go behind over my head certainly would be insubordination, and you *would* answer for that. I shouldn't have to reassure senior staff that I would do nothing to jeopardize our security. If our diplomatic efforts fail and events run beyond our control, it may be necessary to sacrifice Marcin to maintain the balance. When all is said and done, she isn't one of us – and as you have already pointed out, she's nothing but trouble anyway.'

The conflict was written on his face. Perhaps there was some acceptable justification after all. 'So, you're setting her up? And what does she think is happening?'

'If things go wrong, I want her far from here. Far from us. We can say she escaped. Not so far-fetched when you consider the number of delusional fools who have aided and abetted her in the past. It's only a contingency, Thonsen.' Her tone had subtly switched now to reassuring and confiding.

'Why the secrecy?' he asked.

'As I said, she escaped. She may not be one of us, but some of our own still relate to her. The Marcin legend is larger than life. It would be damaging if we were seen to have thrown her to the wolves.'

Every word came with a supporting subliminal narrative... *I'm confiding. You're my friend and ally. I need your support... the right thing... sound judgement.*

'Are we just to keep quiet about her disappearance? People will notice. Rumours will spread.'

'We're counting on it,' she answered. 'Rumour is the best way to leak news of her escape. Obviously, it's not something we would advertise... Was there anything else, Thonsen?'

What else could there be? Thonsen left, his mind more at ease again on one level, almost torn apart on another.

Chapter Five

The sun had slipped behind the mountain three hours ago. It was fully dark now. Mild enough for the season not to have to worry about the cold though. They were supposed to be observing the *Spacer* outpost for unusual activity. Cap was as focused as always. Emii was anything but.

Emii lived for freedom. In moments like this, there wasn't much that could shake her from that. Right here, and right now, there was no immediate menace, no hunger, no cold, and no illness. The past was just the past, and the future was so utterly unfathomable to be a complete waste of energy to even think or worry about. It was a useful character trait for these times, to able to live in the moment.

A gentle night under a starry sky, she thought. Strange how few of us can experience and enjoy such a thing.

Pure unfiltered and unconditioned air caressed her face on the breeze. An almost undetectable and indescribable sound reverberated endlessly into the skies –

the sound of a spinning planet, and its delicately thin and mostly sleeping skin of life.

All the inconvenience, discomfort, unrelenting uncertainty, soul numbing pain of losing people before their time, was the price of a life beyond the crowded artificial hives that hardly troubled the Earth's surface now. As extortionate as that price could seem, no one paid it more gladly than Emii.

'The sky is *so* beautiful. Don't you ever just look at it, Cap?'

'Believe it or not I do, Emii, but not when I'm supposed to be looking at something else.'

'It goes on forever. I wonder how far they'll make it… the *Spacers* I mean.'

'You mean we. How far we'll make it,' Cap corrected.

Emii smiled at that. 'We? We wish. Rockbound is what we are. I wonder if they'll ever forget where they came from, and accidentally find us again one day.'

'You're always wondering about anything but what you're supposed to be wondering about.'

'What else is there to wonder about?'

'Like why a hover waits until the middle of the night before setting out in the opposite direction of the city or the *Island Base*. Like why it hugs the ground in full-dark operation. Like who might be in there, and what they might be up to. It's the second in two days. The first never returned.'

'If they're looking for Stan, that's a good thing, right? Find Stan, find Etta too. They're not going to rescue one and leave the other… not that she's not capable of looking after herself anyway.'

Cap was serious and focused with the LL field magnifier strapped to her head, laying on her belly facing the outpost. 'We have no idea what they're really up to in there, or what their plans are. If they're helping, it's not out of some altruistic desire to do right by us. It would just serve their own interests. Their interests are not necessarily ours… or Etta's. If they bring them here, there might be a chance of seeing them again. If they take them back to the *Island…*' she paused. '… if they take them to the *Island*, they may as well be in space.'

Emii didn't respond immediately. She was almost tempted to ask if it would be such a bad thing. Wasn't that what they all wanted? What they had all practically begged for before?

As if she'd read her mind, Cap pulled the LL unit off and looked at her. 'If we ever go with them, we will all go together, as equals.'

Emii nodded her acknowledgement. 'I know. I know you think I'm away in my own head half the time, but I know that, Cap… I believe we will all go one day. Don't give up on them. I don't believe they have given up on us yet.'

'I admire your optimism, Emii. I wish I was as sure as you.'

'They're still here, Cap. Not just here, but right here where we are. If the *EYE* decided to push them off the map, there wouldn't be much they could do about it either. They have to be careful, like us. And Etta will be fine… she's my sister. Believe me, she'll be fine. She'll be leading us before we know it.'

Now Cap smiled, 'Will she? And what about you? I thought you might want that job. It's not beyond you.'

Emii felt a flush of pride and embarrassment. It had been in the back of her mind for a long time. She had the status and connections. She could almost believe she had the wisdom and the skills. Her younger sister Etta could say the same, but she had something else too; that legendary toughness and resilience – and that other intangible quality – popularity. If and when the time ever came, she would have to convince herself as much as anyone else who was the more worthy.

'Don't worry,' Cap said, 'Helaine will outlast all of us yet. There'll be plenty of time for life to knock the wispy romance out of your head. We're holding a council tomorrow. You shouldn't feel any pressure if you're invited. It isn't a test or an interview. Show that you can listen and speak only if you're asked. I don't think I need to tell you that. I would if I were speaking to Etta. A lot of different qualities go into making a good leader, Emii.'

Emii breathed the night in deeply as she looked up at the stars. She felt surprisingly calm. Cap was right though, there really was no pressure, not yet.

. . .

It was a humbling experience to be in the presence of the people of the council. Their places had all been earned. Their abilities and competences unquestionably demonstrated. They were the safest of safe hands, and they had seen difficult times. She was practically a child here, and when Helaine entered, she realised they all felt the same way in her presence.

Emii had met Helaine several times before. A fact that hardly diminished the effect though. Helaine had the most striking physical presence of anyone she'd ever seen. It wasn't just her stature. She had a strength that could only be described as whole. Even in late middle age, her ultra-dark skin was flawless and radiant. She carried herself proudly and gracefully, majestically even. How could she ever hope to carry off that level of assuredness?

Surprisingly, when she entered there was no ceremony, no regal pauses for admiration and adulation. She simply walked to the front and began speaking.

'Etta isn't coming home.' She stated it without any hint of fear or sadness. 'There is no sense in pretending things are not happening that are beyond our knowledge and control – they are – as they always have.'

Her deep intense gaze missed nothing and swept up everything and everyone in the room.

'So,' she continued, 'what to do? Sit and wait, and hope the answers just come to us? or actively seek them ourselves? These are our options. I propose sending delegations to both the *Eastern Base* of the *Spacers*, and to Neam, to the *EYE* herself. Our situation has been somewhat fluid for a long time... for all time. But there is no need to fear opportunity. How and where we live now has never been a destination. I will not sweeten Etta's current prospects. She may well turn out to be another sacrifice. If it is, hers will not have been the first, and it will not be the last. Do we believe in freedom? If we do not, the *EYE* will welcome our return. If we do, we also believe in sacrifice – past, present, and future sacrifice.'

She gave everyone a moment to digest what she had said so far. The room was silent as each individual reflected quietly.

'I will personally represent us at the Spacers outpost. I don't see much risk when weighed against the possible benefits. The city however is a different proposition. It could be a one-way journey. Whoever goes, you are qualified only by your courage. I ask now for volunteers.'

There was no *think about this and let me know.* That was it. The question had been asked... step forward, or step back.

Surprising even herself, Emii was first to speak without even thinking. 'I will go to the city. I volunteer myself for Neam.'

There were no exclamations from the council. No pats on the back. None of them reacted at all. They waited for Helaine's judgement on the matter.

'We thank you, Emii. I will speak with you alone before you leave. Does anyone object to these proposals or have anything to add at this time?'

They were quiet still. If there was nothing to add, no one here would ever add for adding's sake.

Chapter Six

Evelyn and her team had left in cover of darkness, flying low towards the empty north-eastern wilderness. There was no light anywhere, not from their craft, certainly not from the landscape below. Even the tiniest sliver of a new moon only served to accentuate the blackness. They soon circled clockwise down to the south again though, intersecting the Inter-way a hundred miles south of Neam's perimeter.

Their plan – to intercept a Scheduled Citizen Transfer coming up from Swale, the southernmost of the four cities on this continent.

The vast distances that separated the cities were not coincidental or accidental. Not that it was something their citizens were encouraged to think about. Cities were unlikely to form alliances when they were so physically isolated. The merging, pruning, and rebuilding of the old world, was controlled by the architect of the new one.

The *Spacers*, resourceful and forward thinking as they had always been, at some point had acquired a selection of *SecCore* uniforms. Their plan here was to use that unquestioning citizen programming to make a *selection correction.* Two male citizens would now be required divert to a different city, to be replaced by two new female citizens en route.

In fact, the destinies of those two male citizens would be taking an unimagined and irreversible course change. It didn't really matter so much. It wasn't like they had chosen either destination. When you were selected for the rebalancing program, you were starting a new life anyway; like it or not, ready or not. A year from now they might be starting over on an entirely new world, but at least they might finally have a say in their own lives.

Far from feeling bad for them, Evelyn knew they had the better part of the deal. Going back to the city was the last thing she wanted.

She'd been partnered with a female pilot called Saska, who seemed calm and competent enough. The mystery she intended to ask her about later was how seemingly sensible individuals could be persuaded to do Gaudynya's clearly unsanctioned bidding – even when prospects were as bleak their current situation.

. . .

Etta was pacing, agitated.

'Doesn't it strike you as a strange way to keep two detainees that you just snatched from under your adversary's nose? They haven't even separated us.'

'You know you're popular when your fellow inmate is pushing for solitary confinement over sharing a comfortable residence,' Stan mumbled, laying on his back on an extravagantly upholstered bench.

'I'm not pushing for anything. Maybe this is part of the *EYE's* interrogation strategy. Make us sweat in comfortable surroundings for a while, so the anticipation is worse.'

'Etta, try and relax. Making people comfortable isn't anyone's method of interrogation. I think I know where we are, and probably why. If I'm right, it means we'll be comfortable for some time yet.'

'What do you mean?'

He thought about it. He wanted to reassure her and keep her informed as far as he could. They were allies, and he'd already developed a sense of attachment to her. There were just some things she could never know though.

'I think Evelyn stayed here once, before. It's a long story. Why here? I don't think it's a coincidence. I think we're waiting for her. I think we're probably bait in the trap.'

'She stayed here?' Etta was surprised, and a little impressed. 'This must be the highest of the high and mighty, even for this city. What was she doing here?'

'Yeah, it pretty much is. The residence of a High First Citizen. Someone called, Elleng Ettra. He's dead now though. He was a big name in the early resistance, before there was even anyone living outside. He was the guy who helped get all of that started.'

Etta's demeanour changed. She was seeing with fresh eyes, taking it in. Her hands touched the furniture as she walked. Her head shook slightly in wonder at her own imaginings.

'That history really means something doesn't it? To all of you, I mean.' He already knew it did, but occasionally there was obvious evidence of just how powerful Evelyn's influence had been.

She paused, conflicted. The truth was the only thing she could tell though. 'You don't even know, do you?'

'I have an idea,' he answered calmly.

'You're together, you are the father of her child – and you *have an idea*? Do you know how strange that sounds to us? Everything we've been through, all of it, all of our struggles and sacrifices, everything we are, everything we ever hope to be, was built on her shoulders.'

He felt a fool for sounding as if he'd trivialised it and tried to put it right. 'You're right, I don't really have an idea. Not from your perspective. I know another side of her, from a different place and....' He managed to stop himself from finishing the sentence... *(time)*.

Etta didn't appear to notice. Why would she? She was on a different train of thought now. 'It actually frightens me that she's back, Stan. If the reality doesn't live up to the legend, what are we left with? I feel like it would crush our hearts. I have to hope. I have to believe. And I will believe... all the way to the end.'

Her resolve was obvious and unquestionable.

He watched her as she stared out of the sepia tinted transpane wall at the managed arboretum beyond. He thought of Evelyn standing there years earlier, facing similar impossible odds. Evelyn hadn't been alone then, and neither was Etta now.

'You are what you are, Etta. Everything you've been through and survived, you've been through and survived. Evelyn would tell you exactly the same thing. You owe her nothing... you, are everything. She'll fight for you Etta, don't ever doubt that, and she won't disappoint. But not because you need it – because you're worth it. If you want to believe in something, believe that.'

She turned to face him again, far less hardness in her eyes now. 'Thank you. It's reassuring that she has enough good judgement to choose a good partner at least. I guess that's one less thing to worry about.'

. . .

The Interway became the Mainway as they passed from uninhabited and unmanaged wilderness into the wild Outer Rec zone of the city. The flat route began to carve into the hills rising on either side of them now. A few more miles and they would be passing the ridge where Evelyn had first encountered Helaine. She clearly remembered that meteor-streaked night, pursued under fire to a dawn rebel rendezvous. Her heart ached at how Helaine's must have broken when they finally had to abandon the settlement. It hadn't been much, and always fragile… but it was everything to her. It was a symbol of hope. Now it was lost hope. With her hand resting tenderly on her stomach she wondered again what she was doing here. She could have been home, with Stan. Couldn't they have been happy in ignorance? Couldn't she have just lived with a little nagging doubt?

The Citizen Transfer transport suddenly began to slow, right in the deepest part of the pass. Saska glanced at Evelyn, grave resolve in her eyes, perhaps a silent farewell before a final showdown.

'Have faith, Saska,' she whispered. 'Trust me that there is always a way. Stay calm and follow my lead, ok?'

'Evelyn…'

'Saska, if I tell you that you're going to be alright, you are *going* to be alright.'

'How?'

'You'll see. Trust me.'

They were at a standstill. Two *SecCore* PGV's blocked the way ahead and two groups stood facing them on either side of the road. Each consisted of three individuals immaculately dressed in the brilliant aqua robes of a 1st Citizen, and one in the standard striking black and orange uniform of city *SecCore*.

One of the *Sec's* approached from the front and disappeared from view, presumably entering through the forward cabin.

'Shouldn't we separate? There are only two actual *Sec's*. We should be able to do this,' Saska asked quietly.

Evelyn casually continued to watch the others outside. 'They're not *1st's* Saska, not like you think you know. Those two *Sec's* are the least of our concerns.'

'What do you mean?' she whispered.

'These are something else. They're the *EYE's* elite envoys. Most people don't even know what they do. You're unlucky if you ever meet one, and we have six.'

'So, what do we do?'

Evelyn paused. 'We wait for a fight we can win.'

A brilliant aqua form had appeared now at the front of their own cabin. He was slight in build and almost a senior in age, certainly not physically imposing. It wasn't difficult to imagine what would be going through Saska's mind. Evelyn knew better though. It would be the shortest victory in history.

Her whisper was slow and emphatic. 'Remember what I said, Saska. That is an order.'

He walked by them without any indication of recognition… only a further seven paces though. He turned and retraced his steps out of the cabin.

'That wasn't obvious at all,' Saska whispered.

'Clearly not to you,' Evelyn replied mysteriously.

. . .

Stan and Etta both sat up in attention at the noise. A 1st's arrival was heralded by the unsubtle boots of his accompanying *SecCore* detail. Four of them swept into the room ahead of him with activated N-canes in their hands. They assessed the room before assuming a rehearsed formation with slick and silent efficiency. Two were wide enough to flank them, another two were in front with a three-metre space between, the 1st then capped the reverse-pyramid formation in his aqua-robed brilliance. The formation and its constituents represented pretty much the embodiment of foreboding authority.

Unhurried, the 1st studied his captives carefully before speaking. 'Stan... and Etta.' He directed his gaze to each as he spoke their names, as if telling himself what they were. 'You have been detained by order of the *EYE*. However, I'm sure you recognise that you have been granted enhanced privileges for detainees.'

'Very generous of her,' Stan said. 'And much appreciated.'

'*Very* generous,' Etta echoed with slightly less well disguised sarcasm.

'It is hoped that you will recognise and appreciate the gesture. You are intelligent people. Perhaps you will realise, if not now then later, that mutual accommodation might be beneficial for all of us. Especially as events are still unfolding even as we speak.'

'Unfolding how? Do you really mean unfolding, or do you actually mean you would like them to unfold?' Stan asked, still making a fair effort to keep the sarcastic tone out of his voice.

'There are other interested parties in the current situation. All are shrewd and skilful negotiators. I have direct experience of one though who most definitely is not. One who is predisposed to chaotic spontaneity, some might even say rash behaviour.'

Etta looked at Stan quizzically. 'I wonder who he might be taking about?'

Stan shrugged innocently.

'The fact that someone had a history of clandestine connections within a certain city shouldn't necessarily lead them to assume that those connections still exist. Do you understand what I am saying?' He was looking straight at Stan.

Stan looked at him blankly for a moment, then shrugged again.

'I wanted to make sure that you were aware of the attention to detail,' his eye's rolled around the room, 'and the circumstances of your detention… so that perhaps later you will appreciate the efforts that have been made.'

'I think we recognise them. I definitely appreciate them. Don't you, Etta?'

Etta looked back at him, nodding with undisguised mock sincerity again.

'Don't take it out on Jeremy, Etta. He's made a real effort to explain how well we're being looked after.' He fixed his eyes on her. 'We should show some appreciation. Things could definitely be worse.'

The 1st didn't seem aware or interested in the none too subtle and confusing dramatics between them. 'I will leave you to further convince your colleague of the benefits of cooperation,' he said sternly.

His guard stiffened into even sharper alertness sensing the end of their exchange, conditioned to wordlessly cover his back and retreat in his wake. He wasn't quite finished though.

He looked pointedly at Stan again. 'You might have to be more patient than you would like. Remember though, it *is* a virtue.'

He began to step backwards, then turned and exited through the open archway again, dragging his entourage along behind.

Stan and Etta looked at each other in a silent subliminal exchange before Etta attempted to vocalise their thoughts.

'Just… what? What the rock even was that? I have no idea what just happened,' she said.

'Not much detail obviously, but still more than we have a right to hope for right now. Pretty sure he's for us, and I think he's letting us some kind of network does still exist here. I also think he's trying to warn us about getting too excited about that. And I suspect it was also to give us a heads up that Eve might be about to wade in with something typically inappropriate.'

'So, what does that mean?'

'I think it means that when the shass hits the fan, and it looks like it is going to, we need to be cool. *Be patient,* he said. If things get messy and there is some kind of network left, there might be help for us further down the line. So no Alamo heroics just yet, ok.'

'What's that?'

'A fight we can't win.'

. . .

The black nothingness that had first morphed into a turbulent and disturbing dream-state gradually transformed into a more lucid journey toward consciousness. Evelyn finally started to believe she might be able to open her eyes. Light broke in through one spasming lid, blurry at first, like seeing under water. Then Saska's face slowly came into focus. She looked a good ten minutes ahead in her own recovery, but still very groggy.

'I was beginning to wonder if you were going to make it,' Saska told her sickly.

'I should be so lucky,' Evelyn retorted. 'I take it we managed to bullseye the anticipated pile of shass that was inevitably waiting. What's the story? Where the hell are we even?'

'The blue guy shoved us out and dumped us here. I was just starting to come round at the time. He told me to wait and not move, which considering your condition didn't really seem like an option anyway. Considering my condition it didn't seem like an option. It still doesn't.'

'Good.' Evelyn was sitting up and rubbing the circulation back into her face.

'Good?'

She let out a long exhale after her first deep lungful of fresh air before explaining. 'Sas, we had no plan. Firing ourselves into the city on a Citizen Transfer to and from nowhere was nothing that could ever be considered a plan. You did realise that, right? Our only hope was insider help. I knew it existed once before. I kind of hoped it would still be here... and clearly it is. That's good.'

Saska made a disgusting sound in her throat and spat out a ball of white paste. 'Feel like my insides have been peeled.'

'Please... just don't do that again... ever!'

'Ugh, I know, sorry. I need something to drink. Gaudynya told me you had a plan.'

'I have. You're looking at it, Sas. This is the plan. Welcome to my world.'

'Perhaps I should have asked for details.'

'Yes, perhaps you should,' Evelyn answered sarcastic. 'I was going to ask, and you just reminded me, why the hell everyone does whatever this Gaudynya tells them. Literally nothing about her makes sense. Talk about space-cowboy. She breaks the rules more often than Stan breaks wind. How does she get away with it? You must realise we're not supposed to be here?'

Saska frowned like her head hurt. 'I've worked for her for a long time. I trust her. She gets the job done, Marcin. She looks after her people. She knows what she's doing.'

Evelyn resisted the urge to purge her own throat of its gluey coating. 'Whatever... I'm not buying it, Saska. You can't be that dumb and be a pilot. You can't be that dumb and be anything.'

Saska looked like she might be thinking about it, but whatever it was she shook out from her head. 'What are we going to do now?' she asked.

Evelyn shrugged. 'What the *blue guy* said... we wait.'

Chapter Seven

'Gaudynya is causing havoc down there, you know that?'

Jonas pressed his lips, face set as usual these days in a permanent state of internalised strife. There was plenty to brood about. As Commanding Officer of both Orbiting Stagers, he'd somehow become the go-between for off-world *Spacer* affairs and the precarious presence they still maintained on the planet's surface.

'Would you rather she was back here?'

He asked the question with an unintentional hint of bitterness. It was rhetorical. He knew perfectly well how she would feel about that.

'She's a liability. She's never been anything other than a liability. We will never to be able to use her in any constructive way. It should be clear by now that she's far more adept at using us than we will ever be at using her. And no, Jonas, this is the last place in the universe she should ever be allowed to enter.'

He was starting to lose patience. 'You want me to have her killed. You have difficulty even saying it. Go on, say it. All you have to do is say it, Miik.'

It felt cruel though. He knew how difficult it was. She'd worked alongside Gaudynya for almost a year. He suspected the aftereffects of her exposure ran deeper than any of them acknowledged. Certainly deeper than Miik would want to accept. The changes Gaudynya could exert on a human mind didn't fade the minute you were away from her physical presence. You were left with those alterations. Depending on the length of exposure and the depth and reinforcement of suggestion, they might be irreversible.

Miik kept her tone relatively level. It was an effort not to spit the words out. 'That alone should be a good enough reason to consider it – or has she already stolen your soul too?'

He'd managed to keep Miik operational, albeit in a shielded capacity. Whether it was the right thing to do was just another impossible question for him to brood over. She was damaged, and like it or not, it was irreversible.

She sensed his train of thought and began to lose the battle against frustration. 'Why *have* you kept me here, Jonas? Can either of us go on with the pretence I'll ever be alright?'

He pressed his lips even more. 'Things are what they are, Miik. I know you believe that you're damaged beyond repair. All of us are in a way. It's what life is. Perhaps I was selfish, keeping you so close. I wanted… I *needed* to help you. It's as simple as that.'

He wondered if he should say what he really wanted to say, and then did anyway. 'Perhaps no one can steal my soul when my soulmates with me.'

She was angry, but she almost softened for a second before pushing back – overcompensating against any external influence, well intentioned or otherwise.

She responded to him coldly, 'Unfortunately, platitudes won't help in the current situation. She might be able to see into everyone else's head. None of us can possibly imagine what is in hers now.'

He collected his thoughts. She was right. He did need to focus, separate the emotion from the situation.

'Firstly Miik, I suspect that removing her from her current position may be more difficult than we'd like to believe. The people around her will have been deeply encouraged to defend her – we know that for a fact now. And secondly…' he paused to consider his reasoning. 'And secondly, we need to break our own technological deadlock. As much as we detest the prospect, we need to access a massive volume of raw processing power. We need the *EYE*. We have the foundations, Miik, but that's all. Converting theoretical science into practical, controllable, and useable application, requires something we don't possess. That may take us a hundred years, or it could take half a millennium… and it might not happen at all. What we need is down there. There has to be a way to tap into it.'

She huffed, sarcastic, indignant. 'There is a way. Just bow down to *queen* Gaudynya, or the *EYE,* and start a war between them. Ignore the small matter of our founding principles – freedom, human control, and considerate expansion.'

'Perhaps you're right. It may be the only way. If it is, I hope it's a decision for someone else a long time after I'm gone. I don't want to be the one who trades freedom for endless hollow expansion. I have just the smallest gut feeling that there might be another way yet though.'

It sounded almost like a question, wondering if she understood his meaning, wondering if she might feel it too.

'Oh, yes, *her*. The special one. The legend. The mythical priestess of *Infinity*.'

She wasn't in the mood to hide her contempt for Evelyn Marcin.

'She's a brand for the disenfranchised, nothing more. Has anyone in history been so overrated? If the Marcin woman figures in your reckoning, we may as well all return to the citadels and beg forgiveness of the *EYE*.'

Clearly, she didn't then, and seemed unlikely to be convinced. Perhaps he was trying to convince himself.

'You might be right again. Let me ask you though, who put those words in your mouth? You knew who I was talking about. You called her *special*. You called her *legend*.'

'Because everyone does.'

'Yes, everyone does – including the *EYE*. She has history there too. She has its… respect. Who has ever gone against that and survived? There's something in it, Miik. She has a kind of connection, I'm sure of it.'

It was Miik's turn to capitalise on an opportunity for cruelty. '…because your father believed it. He practically founded this insane religion. Are you going to allow sentiment to influence your judgement?'

Her coldness had stung him in a rare moment of vulnerability. He burned for retaliation, escalation, a full-blown fight. The only outward sign of his irritation though was the tapping of his fingertips on the console.

'You should be envious of his conviction, Miik. At least he believed in something.'

. . .

Gaudynya had clashed with Thonsen twice in one morning. Their last conversation had been brief, but it had still taken its toll. He'd arrived at her quarters with a renewed will and a determination to bring her down – despite her earlier work. Modifying emotions in the moment over trivial issues required concentration. Converting deep-seated resentment and suspicion required a level of focus so intense it was exhausting. In truth, it was impossible… more an unstable mix of deflection and misdirection. Thonsen had a strong mind, and a hardwired sense of mistrust. Keeping all that at bay was more akin to flood defence.

Just walking back to her quarters was an effort. She fought the urge to stop and lay down where she was. She could have slept on the floor. She hardly noticed the man who had turned into the corridor ahead. He didn't feel right, but did she need to do this now? Did she need to summon that energy right now? Sensing accurately was an effort at the best of times.

Behind him, Rianne, one of her own closest and most loyal aids appeared, eyes manically wide. She was charging forward, screaming. Clenched in her white-knuckled right-hand was a kitchen blade. The man turned at the cry and Gaudynya noticed the N-cane previously hidden behind his back. Realisation dawned, but the raw emotional chaos was head-splittingly overwhelming. Her arms flailed as she backed away from the unfolding catastrophe. Rianne silenced with gut wrenching finality as she entered the kill field. She crumpled to the floor with blade sliding uselessly ahead of her. Gaudynya tried to run. There was no plan, only terror… her own and ambient…

...Then there were shadows – people, bodies, faces... Spinning, head-wrecking confusion... Blackness...

. . .

Jonas stood at the back behind the security detail he had ordered to arrest his catastrophically damaged former partner. It was painful but he needed to be there. He didn't even know why. He felt responsible somehow. He always *was* responsible. The circumstances that had led them here were no one's fault. Perhaps he should have seen it coming though.

It had been a crude attempt, and luckily it had failed. He shook his head thinking of the damage she might have done. Gaudynya had almost certainly been alerted to their knowledge of her ability now, and one of their few trusted people on the ground had been exposed. The whole situation was a mess.

Miik's sullen gaze rested on him as the guards ran through their formalities. He stared back at her. There was so much he wanted to say, but so little point now.

. . .

Gaudynya opened her eyes in the medical suite. One minute there had been nothing, the next she was back. It didn't feel like sleep. There was no dream to remember. Her eyes simply opened to reveal the world outside. She stayed where she was, knowing the process of repair was probably still underway. There was no one else in the room anyway.

Her thoughts turned to what was happening in the wider world, beyond the room. Was she a patient, or a prisoner? Had the threat passed? Marcin must certainly be in the city by now. Had something happened there?

A male medi-tech entered. 'Commander. Welcome back. How are you feeling now?'

She allowed her senses to gently explore his emotional state.

No sense of tension or deception. Seems genuinely pleased I'm awake. No need to go any deeper here.

'I'm fine. Tell me what happened,' she ordered aloud.

'I don't know the details of the *incident* if that's what you're referring to. Better your security team brief you accurately on that. Some interesting medical observations though.'

She panicked. How long had she been out? How much diagnostic work had he done? For all she knew she could have been in a coma for weeks.

'How long was I out?' she asked casually.

He was reading data on a wall mounted display and didn't look round. 'About twelve hours from the initial collapse. You came round a couple of times in a state of delirium. We sedated you so you could rest while we made sure there was nothing nasty or ongoing.'

'And?'

'Clearly you suffered no direct brain injury of the type you would in the field of an N-cane. We wouldn't be speaking like this if you had. No toxins. No pathogens. No physical trauma. From what little I've heard though, the shock of the incident itself could be enough to account for the distress and confusion.'

She allowed her eyes to close as she reached a little deeper to check for herself. 'So I'm fine?'

'I don't think there is anything to worry about…'

'…But?'

'…there were some unusual anomalies in your neural output. It's worth monitoring and looking into further.'

Even as he was speaking the idea was seeming less relevant and appealing to him. Probing just a little deeper now, she subtly replaced his concerns with more positive emotions. It wasn't as difficult as she feared it might be.

'I think we both know I'm fine now, if a little embarrassed. Let's not waste more time on unnecessary tests. I was tired. I have been under extra pressure lately. Clearly the trauma brought things to a head. I'll definitely be more careful with my schedule from now on.'

His will to please her was already strong enough to pre-empt her wishes now. 'I'll make sure you are allowed to rest a little longer. And no need for embarrassment. All anyone needs to know is that you're fit for duty.'

'Thank you,' she smiled.

Chapter Eight

An agricultural workforce transporter appeared in the distance. A brilliant star of low afternoon sun reflected off the front shield as it glided smoothly and silently toward them.

'Déjà vu,' Evelyn whispered to herself.

'What's that?' Saska asked.

'It means it's time to get up, Sas. We need to smarten ourselves and not look like we just came back from the dead. This is probably our ride. Look as if we're having a chat and don't show any interest in it. If it stops, follow my lead… and keep your mouth shut.'

It slowed as it approached.

'Remember,' Evelyn reminded her quietly, 'we're not interested… we might be waiting for someone else for all they know… we're not even looking at it… ok, here it comes.'

'Yes, I do remember,' Saska replied in over-acted conversation. 'See how much I'm not looking at it, even though I'm actually *very* interested to find out what the rock is going on.'

The heavily tinted entryway slid open. Evelyn half expected to see the same fresh face she had once before in an eerily similar situation. To her frustration his name escaped her now, probably because of the drugs, but she remembered the face. It was a different one that greeted them this time, another young man. He didn't speak, but his eyes flicked in what she took to be a *follow me* gesture. Saska stayed close on her heals as she stepped aboard and made her way to a pair of vacant seats. Then the transporter, with its unnaturally subdued human cargo, accelerated silently on its way again. The silence culture was no surprise to Evelyn. It was something she had switched in and out of many times before. It would be strange for Saska though. She would be aware of that undercurrent of awkwardness and tension more than anyone. At least it made it easier to blend in. All they had to do was be quiet.

At the changeover station, Evelyn knew the drill. She stayed in her seat, paying close attention to an imaginary footwear issue as the workforce filed out for another day that would be the same as the last, and the next – until their scheduled rotation at least. Evelyn's footwear issue was sufficiently interesting for Saska to be fascinated by it too. Perhaps the young man also had a pressing footwear issue of his own to deal with. He remained seated.

'Well, has anything changed at all since my last visit?' she asked him when they were alone. 'I take it we're going to have the usual run around to the latest hub of resistance.'

He was surprisingly short with her. 'Everything has changed. There's no resistance to speak of for one thing. There'll be no *run around* either. What you need is here or it is nowhere.'

Clearly, he wasn't as awed by her presence as the young man who had helped her before. His name suddenly came back to her.

'Enstae.' She said aloud, but to herself.

The look she got was less than warming.

'I'm glad you remember his name at least, seeing as that's all there is left.'

The words were like a blow to the stomach. Her encounter with Enstae had been brief, but lifesaving. He'd risked everything to help her when she needed it the most, without even knowing or having met her before. He'd saved her life, and eventually it must have cost him his own.

'I'm sorry to hear that. I can't even tell you how sorry. He was a good man. I understand if you will not offer your own name. I am Evelyn Marcin, and I am as grateful to meet you as I was Enstae.'

Saska remained quiet. She had no part in this. After the short exchange though he seemed to accept them. Possibly only Evelyn Marcin could have said what he had needed to hear.

'My name is Yonji Ensza. You are my cause. One way or another, my life is never my own. Better it belongs to you than the *EYE*.'

She nodded respectfully. 'Tell us what we're to do, Yonji.'

'Someone is waiting. If you follow me, you will meet with him. My part is only to show you the way.'

'Ok, you lead. We'll follow.'

Rising from his seat he gave his own short sincere bow before setting out ahead of them.

The section he led them to was on an underground level, an interior four room complex built into the corner of storage bay that looked unused and forgotten.

He stopped at the entrance. 'You may go inside now. The contact is unsecured.'

'Do you want me to take a look first?' Saska offered.

'We're safe enough, Sas,' Evelyn replied looking at Yonji. 'We'll go in together.'

They stepped in as the doorway slid opened and it closed automatically behind them. The room was clean and brightly lit, in contrast with its exterior. It seemed it might be a workforce briefing area. The front quarter was raised up a step and faced five rows of moulded seating. Another doorway opened opposite, revealing a man dressed in the distinctive aqua robes of a 1st citizen. He walked seriously and very directly straight up to Evelyn, stopping unsociably and uncomfortably close to her.

She smiled warmly at him. 'It doesn't work on me. I wrote the book on antisocial, remember? Nice to see you again, Jeremy.'

He stepped back to a more comfortable distance, smiling too. 'Alive at least ...for now.'

The memory of his unique ability came back to her, and she felt a moment of panic. 'Are you still...?'

'...Connected? Things are a little different now. Let's just say I'm awaiting my upgrade.'

'So we're alone? The *EYE* is unaware of this?'

'We're fine. Which is more than I can say for some others. Getting you here was more difficult than you know. You should be glad you were out for most of it.'

'Dare I ask?'

'No,' he replied, looking like he meant it.

There was an awkward pause. Both seemed at a loss of how to continue.

Saska tried to ease things along. 'You know each other, and you have a lot to catch up on. You can't do it all at once. Someone just needs to make a start here.'

Jeremy smiled again. 'Indeed. I know why you're here of course, Evelyn. It doesn't take a genius or a friend to work it out. You didn't come back to change the world and save us ...you're here for Stan.'

She gave the old trademark shrug. 'I never claimed to be anyone's saviour. Yes, I do want him back, and the more you can help with that, the less mess I'll make.'

He looked wise and a little sad as he considered their situation and what to say to her. 'The horse that won't drink ...isn't that what Elleng used to call you?'

He sat resting his elbows on his knees. 'You never seem to know even half the story, and yet you always drop into it like a grenade.'

'That's low for you, bringing Elleng into it. I'm not abandoning anything. You're right, I know half of zero, so help me get Stan and we'll work something out.'

'It's too late to figure out how this is will go, Evelyn. It's already going. Stan is bait on the hook. The *EYE* always did have an odd fascination for you. She wants you, o*nly* you ...and they probably want rid of you.' He looked at Saska as he said that. 'If you're not careful you might find yourself fighting everyone here without any cause or benefit.'

'What else can I do? It's what I do.'

Saska interrupted, indignant, 'Excuse me. I didn't risk my life breaking into the city to get *rid* of anyone.'

'No, you didn't,' Jeremy explained patiently. 'You risked your life because someone told you to, and I think we all know who that someone was.'

Saska's cheek twitched involuntarily. Evelyn sensed he was arriving at his point. '…Gaudynya?' she asked.

Saska interrupted again defensively, 'She is my commander. I follow the orders of my commander. I put my life at risk, for my commander. That's hardly a telling revelation.'

The pieces were starting to fall into place now for Evelyn. '…Even if it goes against the very foundations of the people you represent – The *Spacers'* founding principles. …Even if the stakes are as high as risking a war or being banished from your home-world.'

She closed her eyes, massaging her temples. 'How could I have needed someone to point this out to me? Is there something wrong with me too?'

Jeremy shrugged. 'Perhaps, but it's unlikely you're affected to the same degree.'

Saska was growing impatient and even more paranoid. 'What in space are you two talking about? Can you hear yourselves?'

'You know it makes sense. You do whatever she says. Look around, Saska. Look at where you are. Think about what we're doing here.'

'You think she's controlling me? Controlling my mind?'

The reply was silence, the most convincing evidence they could give. They didn't need to persuade her, just give her time to think it through.

Eventually Jeremy broke it. 'It's the new way. Gaudynya was one of the first. There are many more now. In truth I have no idea how many. All the new envoys are prepped this way. It's what makes me more or less obsolete.'

'Ok, so what is it? What does the *EYE* do to them?'

'Artificial Intelligence meet Artificial Biology. Self-replicating bio-machines with a range of functions. They embed into the body's own systems to modify and protect them. The neural ones amplify and enhance specific brain inputs and outputs to create a powerful subliminal communication tool. I believe it works on an emotional level, which is what makes it so effective ...and dangerous. Most behaviours have emotional triggers. Control the emotion – you control the behaviour. The purpose is to allow the *EYE* to manipulate individuals directly, but eventually it seems some individuals can become adept at using it for their own ends.'

Saska looked cold and Evelyn felt for her. It must seem like the worse kind of harm. One that could reach down and alter the core of your own true self. One that could turn you inside out and change you into anything it wanted.

Jeremy continued on unmoved. 'If you have the neural implants, it seems you're on a timer. When you begin to use it creatively, she decommissions you. I'm not exactly sure why yet.'

Evelyn thought about that. 'So what does that make Gaudynya? An experiment gone wrong? Frankenstein's monster?'

He looked down at the floor as he remembered the order of events ...and all that came with the memories. 'We always knew there was a possibility the *EYE* would rescind our concessions at some point. In anticipation of that we maintained a covert chapter of the old resistance. Gaudynya contacted us. She needed a way out and asked for our help. That was just before the *EYE* isolated the settlement and locked the city down again. I suspect the Gaudynya situation was the catalyst for that. Something about her was different, even for an enhanced envoy

...something that had the *EYE* spooked. What little we know about the program is information obtained directly or indirectly from Gaudynya.'

'What do you think it was?' Saska asked him. 'What about her could possibly spook the *EYE?*'

'At the time, Gaudynya was shaken. She was afraid. There seemed an urgency to get out of the city as quickly as possible. Bear in mind she was a capable influencer even then, but she did mention something about an *Apex routine*. It was clearly the source of her troubles. It was never explained to us in enough useful detail though.'

'Lots of things we might be tempted to infer though, from what you've told us,' Evelyn offered.

'Possibly...' He shrugged again and waited.

She followed her own logic. 'Like you're telling us all of this ...why? You intercept our half-assed doomed rescue mission ...why? ...Because we're old friends? ...Or because of our possible connection back to Gaudynya and whatever this *Apex* can mean for you?'

He smiled resignedly. 'Yes, and for all the reasons you know. We're running out of road and heading for the cliffs again. You make things happen, Evelyn. Things happen around you. It's inexplicable, but I've seen it. We're desperate enough to believe in that magic again. Current tensions are set to tear us apart. Perhaps you can fix it. If anyone can, I actually believe you can.'

She sighed with her hand on her belly. *I wonder if you'll have to live with this curse of unreasonable expectations.*

'Help me get Stan. If you can do that, we'll see what kind of a spell I can whip up this time.'

He nodded, but he also spread his palms in a gesture that suggested he was less than hopeful. 'There's a low probability of success, even with my help. Any hope you represent could be lost for the sake of one impossible mission to recover two low priority people ...but you already know that.'

'Impossible is my middle name, lost causes my speciality. If it's what you need, it's what I've got ...so buckle up.'

And you buckle up too junior. You're going to have to get used to this I'm afraid.

. . .

Gaudynya lay in her darkened quarters, still recovering from the effects of her earlier overload. Things were still under control on the ground. The situation was clearly developing above though, off-world, their botched assassination was evidence of that. It would only be a matter of time before they looked for an alternative method of removal.

But trouble was always an opportunity. It was what she wanted. Chaos. It was coming. And when it did, and when everyone else was lost in its storm, she would finally be home.

Chapter Nine

'I don't think this is a good time to be visiting the *Spacers*, Helaine. *SecCore* forces are everywhere. There are two main concentrations directly east and west of the base now, and a full perimeter of sentry units. It may be a show of strength, a threat, or this could be it …a clear-out of all opposition to the all-power of the *EYE*,' Cap advised.

Helaine stared over the low hills, her face dark and thoughtful. Her calm brown eyes never betrayed her with worry or fear, only the capacity to match anything life could throw at her. She stood silent and strong.

'What do you want us to do?' Cap asked.

She was silent still, even though she was clearly present and attentive, eyes scanning the landscape almost as if she were communing with it.

Cap was growing impatient at being ignored though. 'Helaine. What do…'

'You're right,' she interrupted. '…it *is* time.'

Cap shivered. Goose bumps raised under her hair. 'What does that mean?'

'Are you ready to fight, Cap? Are you ready to give your life to a *human* cause?'

Cap filled her chest and answered, 'A question you never need ask. A question I'll never ask of you.'

Helaine nodded, unsmiling, face hard against the cold gusts that were testing her eyes now. '...and the *Corps*?'

Cap took the time to find the right words that fit the gravity of the question. 'We've all lost someone, we've all felt the cold, and we have all stayed strong. We all know there's no going back ...and perhaps no way forward, but the *Corps* will fight the *EYE* to its last breath, Helaine Tangela.'

'We should prepare ourselves then.'

. . .

Etta and Stan had been treated well. Things could have been much worse, and they had expected them to be. They had the extravagant luxury of twice daily showers and fresh clothing; more than either was used to or felt necessary, but it was a break from the boredom. They had excellent meals too. There had been no more enigmatic visits from strange *1st's*. The only people they saw were the regular *SecCore* guard, at mealtimes, or if they strayed to the boundaries of their 'territory'.

Stan couldn't explain it, but he had a feeling this day was going to be different. Maybe they would finally be separated and interrogated as they had expected ...or maybe a doorway would shatter into million pieces to reveal a petit, stern faced, sable haired warrior with a cannon strapped to each arm.

When it came, it wasn't quite so dramatic …at first. The usual boot-fall down the hallway heralded the arrival of the imposing black and orange uniforms that assumed a formation as they stamped in through the archway, followed by the vibrant dayglow aqua of their accompanying *1st* envoy, floating grandly behind.

The scene before Stan and Etta, when it registered, was so surreal it almost felt almost like comedy. Evelyn was dressed in *SecCore* colours and standing to attention behind Jeremy's formal aqua brilliance. Her face was fixed and neutral, eyes not meeting anyone's.

Jeremy announced with authority, 'You will be haloed for transfer as a precaution. Considering the comforts you have been afforded so far, I'm sure it should hardly be necessary. It is standard transfer protocol.'

Evelyn and her *SecCore* 'partner' Saska moved forward, haloes in hand. As she gently secured Stan, Saska attended to Etta. It took all of his concentration to stay focused. He wanted to laugh, but mostly he wanted to hold her and lift her off her feet. He wanted to breathe her in and kiss her. Etta was just as distracted and self-conscious too. When they were ready, Jeremy stepped aside, and the formation opened up to let them through. With a hand on his upper arm, Evelyn pushed Stan through the gap. Etta and her *guard* followed. Jeremy fell in behind and the rest of the unit collapsed into three pairs at the back.

Stan tried his best to look sullen, and found it wasn't so hard as Evelyn prodded him along the corridor. It was all too easy in fact. Too good to be true. Evelyn was far from stupid, but she wanted to believe this would work …and that was his fault. He realised he was preparing for the inevitable, her failure. A fear worse than any *SecCore* could imbue.

Another aqua 1st appeared directly ahead of them, not phased remotely by the scene that confronted him. Jeremy's face also gave nothing away.

'A disappointing development, Jeremy, but not entirely unexpected,' he said.

Jeremy spoke calmly. 'I appeal directly to the will of the *EYE*. Let Starmun step aside. No good will come of Evelyn Marcin's presence in this city.'

Starmun replied simply, 'No.'

Jeremy stepped forward to stand toe to toe with Starmun, but with no aggression in his body language. His face was calm – and sad. His demeanour was almost submissive.

Then suddenly fear registered in Starmun's eyes, before any move was even made. Jeremy's skilfully masked intention had been impossible to contain any longer. Beneath the folds of his gown the field of the N-cane activated, causing Starmun to slump like his soul had left his body.

There was a moment's pause as eleven minds processed what had happened. The *SecCore* unit probably felt the shock the most. On some level they were perhaps more aware of Starmun's mental presence – the one dramatically yanked from existence. By the time they were coming to their senses, the first was already on the floor. Saska's foot had flicked directly under his chin, snapping his head back, and Stan had already rammed his haloed head into the face of another before reaching for the throat of his next target. Evelyn's elbow also connected with an unsuspecting jaw before spinning on to another. With the six neutralised *SecCore* on the ground, Saska felt for a grip on one of their dazed heads from behind. Evelyn watched her take a hold of his chin and screamed in realisation.

'No!'

Saska looked up, eyes wild.

'No, Saska!'

'How far will we get with these behind us?' she gasped.

'I don't care. We get as far as we get without murdering people.'

Jeremy interjected calmly. 'Can I suggest we leave now.'

They followed as he led the way through the mansion, eventually into the open air again. It seemed unnaturally and surreally calm ...but it wouldn't be for long!

'This PGV doesn't track,' he told them. 'There are plenty of other ways we can be picked up though. The chances of getting out of here are slim. I never suggested they would be anything other.'

Evelyn jumped in the front. 'One thing at a time. Just get us to that damned hover, Jeremy.'

They crammed in, tense and breathing hard, a sense of there being no way back now for any of them.

so what's new?

The laneways were clear, but why wouldn't they be? They were heading for the relatively quiet area of the city-service hangers – an open area, sandwiched between northern Agriculture and the Outer Residentials. The main access was from south-central. They all had the feeling things were progressing too easily, even at this stage. Not that there was any point in worrying about it, it wasn't like they had a backup plan.

The northern boundary of the hanger area appeared open, marked only by sporadic low-charge barrier beacons. There was generally no need for anything more substantial. The barrier's only purpose was to deter the wildlife permitted for ecological reasons in the Agricultural zone. Passing through the increasingly resistant field would be uncomfortable, but not unbearable for a human being.

'Where is ours?' Evelyn asked Jeremy, looking beyond the field.

'Forty-eight, practically at the centre,' he replied.

She shook her head in frustration. 'Of course it is. Did I think it would be right in front of us on the north edge. I guess the hover will be shackled too. Do we have a plan for that?'

'You *need* to have a plan for that,' Saska advised. 'I can't just lift off and rip them out. Shacks are a pre-powerup protocol. I can't initiate converters until they're deactivated.'

'It will be taken care of,' Jeremy answered coolly before stepping into the field.

His body tensed visibly as he progressed, making his stride look robotic. He was walking like a zombie.

Stan was half amused, half horrified. 'Great place to put a dance floor. Can I just walk home …that way?'

'You know what I'm going to say, Stan,' Evelyn advised, giving him the tilted head look.

'Yeah, I know that look. If I don't stop complaining, that field's going to be the least of my problems, right?'

'That's right, kiddo.'

'And what about junior?' He looked down at her stomach. 'Is he going to be alright with this?'

They hadn't spoken about it yet. It had felt like she'd known for ages before. Now it was like *he'd* known for ages without her knowing. They looked at each other, trying to fit an hour-long conversation into a subliminal instant.

'I didn't know you knew,' she said gently. 'But there's a lot of stuff *she's* going to have to get used to.'

'There's a lot of stuff *we're* going to have to get used to – like mentioning minor details – like we're going to have a kid.'

Etta had been silent since the breakout from Elleng's old mansion. 'You two are unbelievable,' she whispered.

It sounded tetchy, and like it was mostly directed at Stan. She strode away after Saska, who was already wading like she'd borrowed someone else's legs.

'Etta, right?' Evelyn teased. 'Doesn't look as if things were too uncomfortable…until I turned up at least.'

Stan, looking flustered, had all the encouragement he needed to start moving.

'Slow it down big foot. Don't leave your *family* behind.'

Once through, they jogged after Jeremy past the maze of gunmetal grey cubes that housed individual hover transports. The ones in the centre were all the same size, housing standard light-industrial craft, the city-manufactured workhorse of the *EYE*. The transports used by the *Spacers* were basically the same, albeit with a few modifications to enable maintenance without assistance from the city, or the *EYE*. In the distance on the Eastern edge were the enormous terminals that contained the large Intercontinental Passenger Exchange (IPE) craft. A sight to behold. Evelyn thought she'd seen one close up once, as an infant. A surreal image from her primordial brain soup. It felt like a mixture of memory and imaginings from another life. Even in that *other life* though, there were no faces to be recognised, no parents, no attachments …just those distant grey hangers that brought a feeling of hollowness. It was a feeling she'd almost forgotten. She shook herself out of it and realised she'd just stopped, standing with her hand on her stomach.

Stan placed his hand on top of hers. His eyes were full of concern and compassion. 'It's alright, Eve. Wherever you came from, you're not on your own now and you're never going to be again ...and no man or machine is going to take *our* child away.'

She placed her other hand on top of his. Looking past him she could see Etta, and fifty metres beyond her, Saska and Jeremy. They were waiting patiently for *her*, and she knew they would wait as long as she needed. The black hole had been defeated again, with a little help. She forced a smile, wiped her eyes and nodded. Stan was trying to pull her along gently, but she found herself resisting.

'I will always be home now, Stan, wherever I am, and that's because of you. Never forget that, ok.'

She didn't know why she'd felt the need to say anything. It had just come out.

He nodded. 'I won't. Come on, we need to go.'

They were moving again, their strange interlude left behind. A few minutes later they were at the entryway to hanger forty-eight, with Jeremy producing a thumb size piece of hardware from the folds of his robe. A holo display appeared above it. He deftly moved the shapes of light with a fingertip causing them to migrate from a grid to a circle above. The entry slid open.

He looked at Saska. 'You have full access, and the shackles are deactivated.'

She made her way inside in pilot mode, habitually checking the crafts exterior. Evelyn held back to let the others go ahead, which of course no one did.

'Ladies first,' Stan gestured.

She stayed where she was.

'Oh space, here it comes,' whispered Etta. 'We knew it couldn't be this easy.'

'What the hell's going on?'

She was looking at Jeremy. 'I think you have something to say, and I think now's the time to say it, Jeremy.'

She recognised the look on his face. She'd seen it before, a long time ago, and she'd already noticed it again today, just after abandoning the PGV.

'Freedom always comes at a price, Evelyn. No should understand that better than you.'

Stan stepped toward him, but she calmly put a hand on his chest.

'You two-faced blue turd,' he growled.

'…and that price would be what?' she asked.

'Gaudynya, obviously.'

Evelyn shrugged. 'Fine by me. You can have her. I'll bring her manipulating head back on a popsicle stick if you let us out of here. *I* have no love for her.'

That look was on his face again though. It was a look of conflicted concentration – concentrating on the voice in his head – the *voice* of the *EYE*.

'It isn't that simple, I'm afraid. You're aware of her ability, her power of influence. It's too strong to just go in there and take her out, and the *EYE* doesn't want her back here either.'

'Just tell me what she does want then.'

'It's more a case of what you need – the tools for the job.'

There was no one of an inadequate level of intelligence here. The realisation dawned on them simultaneously.

Etta, 'Not going to happen.'

Stan, 'No way, blue. Not in a million years.'

Saska, 'Let's just go. I can get us out of here right now.'

Jeremy was relaying the words of the *EYE* directly in the first person now, something Evelyn had never seen him do before. Previously he had just conveyed the messages in his own words. 'No, you cannot. I have the capacity to deactivate the craft remotely during operation.'

'What's with this first-person *EYE* bullshass, Jeremy. It's like you've been possessed. Are you still in there? So much for the redundant connection.'

His eyes refocused. 'I'm fine. This is complicated. She needs to speak to you, and you need to speak to her. It's easier for me just to relay this directly.'

'So, what exactly are you proposing?' She was asking the *EYE* directly now.

'That you also receive the conversion.'

Stans hands went to his head and stayed there like they were holding it on. 'That's a flat no, Eve. I'll take the damned conversion. You can't. Not now.'

Etta stepped up too. 'No. I should take it.'

But Jeremy was shaking his head sadly. The words were the *EYE's*, not his own. 'It can only be Evelyn Marcin.'

She felt that black hole again, that gnawing void of the past. Tip of the tongue knowledge that refused to go any further.

'Who would have guessed,' she said quietly. 'Two billion to one and I win again. The *EYE's* right Stan, it can only be me. Can we let them go now, Jeremy?'

He nodded solemnly. 'They can leave, but you won't like that either. They can't go to the *Spacer* base. It would alert Gaudynya to our plans. She wants them to go to the *Outsiders* and find Helaine. It's possible we will need their help soon. She needs to be ready.'

'Will you do that, Saska?' Evelyn asked her.

Saska nodded, uncomfortable.

'Saska,' Evelyn's voice took on a more caring tone. '*Can* you do that? I know it will be difficult.'

Saska nodded again, more positive. 'It will be, but yes, I can do it. Pretty sure these two will incentivize me if I waver. That bitc…'

She stopped herself. She couldn't even say it. It was progress that she wanted to though.

Evelyn turned her attention to Etta. 'I want to thank you for saving Stan's ass so far. I'd be grateful if you could keep him alive a little longer. I need someone to change diapers.'

Etta shrugged. 'I'm under orders from my actual commander, so it's still my job.'

'Don't worry, Etta, he'll earn his keep with what's coming your way.'

Stan was waiting for his turn. No joking around, and no anger now either. 'Go do what you do. Then get your ass back as soon as you can.'

'Remember what I said,' she told him, taking his hands.

Chapter Ten

Gaudynya had learned that in most cases there was no need to fabricate scenarios to modify or reinforce a person's behaviour. It could be done against the background of everyday life. In fact, in most cases it was easier if the subject was distracted in conversation with someone else.

This was not such a case. The *SecCore* commander, Verrana Rhone, was usually beyond casual reach, and meetings were risky. On the plus side though, the job was made easier by a barely containable mutual attraction. The only complications were logistical, covering their tracks to rendezvous beyond the base barrier and *SecCore* surveillance. Gaudynya expended more energy manipulating a window of opportunity than she ever needed to use manipulating Verrana. Her efforts were usually more physical in nature anyway.

'I'm always jealous of your Spacer uniform, Gaudynya. Few wear it so well though.'

'You don't have to pretend to be nice to me, Verrana. I know you're here to demand my unconditional surrender …again!'

Verrana smiled and stroked a lock of Gaudynya's hair. 'I just might, if you're good. Perhaps we can both surrender this time.'

Gaudynya smiled, biting her lip sensuously. 'We need to talk a little business first.'

'User. Come on, out with it. We never have enough time as it is.'

She paused to make herself appear vulnerable, then said, 'I'm in danger, Verrana. I'm afraid.'

Verrana's mood switched instantly and visibly. She was shaken at the thought. 'You should come with me. I'll work something out. I'll look after you. I can't protect you in there.'

'I would be in even more danger. The *EYE* wants to hurt me too, Verrana. She will do anything. If you won't kill me, she'll find someone who will.'

Verrana smiled nervously. 'Someone else? Who? I've practically annexed her entire regional ground forces. Between me, your own people, and your own aircraft, you are virtually untouchable.'

'What about the *Outsiders*?'

Verrana looked incredulous. 'The *Outsiders*? They are nothing. They would be no match for us. Why would they even try? And surely, they would feel more allegiant to you than the *EYE*. I think they have enough worries of their own anyway without starting fights they can't possibly win.'

'The *EYE* is the ultimate authority when it comes to manipulation, Verrana …and now she has leverage.'

'Leverage? What leverage, Gaud? What could the *EYE* offer that the outsiders would want or believe?'

'The one thing they need. The one thing they do believe in – their saviour – their *Queen* …she has her.'

'I understand you even less. Who? Helaine? They will just elect another. Their objective is to live outside, not die outside. I hardly think they would lead a suicidal assault on your base at the request of the *EYE*.'

'I'm not talking about Helaine ...I'm talking about Evelyn Marcin.'

Verrana stood open-mouthed for a moment. The name didn't have the same emotional context for her as it would an *Outsider*, but it was a name she knew well enough. Every thought, memory and emotion Verrana had of Marcin was reinforced or suppressed by Gaudynya as it arose, until finally she allowed her to reply. 'I can see how that might change things. It doesn't alter the fact that they simply do not have the capability to threaten you.'

Gaudynya made her face grave and vulnerable, the method actress. 'I hoped you of all people wouldn't underestimate the power of love ...and make no mistake, Verrana, they do love her.'

It only needed the smallest push now to make her say what she wanted to hear. 'If it's their love for her against my love for you, you have nothing to fear. This is our life now. We have each-others backs. We have *each other*, Gaud.'

Gaudynya sat down on the ground, vulnerable. She held up her hand, smiling submissively. 'Show me, Verrana. Show me you love me.'

. . .

'You alright there, Saska?' Etta asked.

She'd been watching her every second since take off. It was only a short flight to freedom and Saska was going to be acutely aware of that fact. If part of her felt there was still a choice to make, this was her opportunity.

'I won't lie, Etta, this is every kind of wrong for me. I have no idea what I'm doing right now. I'm just focusing on getting this bird down before I throw up. After we land, you should just shoot me. I might just shoot myself.'

Stan wasn't in the best frame of mind to be offering encouragement. Ironically, it was just what she needed though. 'You're not alone, Saska. I am though. Maybe I'll join you. Maybe we can do ourselves a favour and shoot each other.'

Etta shook her head. 'Good talk. Last week I was babysitting. This week its suicide watch. If this turns out to be a waste of time, *I'll* shoot you both.'

Saska smiled first, then Stan, and then finally even Etta.

'So, anyway, where exactly am I putting us down, Etta?'

'Nav up, I'll show you. I'm going to give us a little walking time. Things as they are, a strange H dropping in might be cause for concern. Accidents happen when people are on edge. It's not something we boast about, but we do have limited ground to air options. I don't want to test its effectiveness.'

Stan was surprised and mildly impressed. 'Yeah, let's not test that. I do miss the days when I could get dropped off outside my home at any time of day or night though.'

'What the rock are you griping about now?'

He shook his head moodily.

'Five minutes your feet will be back on the ground. Try not to worry. Evelyn will… She…'

Etta and Stan looked at each other. The conflict in Saska was painful to watch. The moment was awkward for all of them. They were conflicted too, between compassion for her and concern for their own lives.

Etta reacted with typical directness. 'We don't have to pretend this isn't weird, Saska. Clearly this is difficult for you. If you want my advice, just focus on what you're doing. Don't get hung up on who's side you're on, who's right, who's wrong, who you do or don't like, or why. Only time is going to work that out for you.'

Stan stared outside. *Why do people think time makes everything alright? Time can't fix the mess they make of your head.*

They set down on a stony clearing on a low hill. On landing the deep hum of the six converters cut instantly, leaving a vacuum of sound that confused the senses.

Stan looked at Etta in the odd silence. 'Shall we? …after you.'

Saska unbuckled and Etta activated the gullwing, not even bothering to lower the ramp before jumping out. Stan jumped out after her. The gullwing then began to lower back into position. He had just enough time to shout to Saska before it sealed.

Etta was shouting too, more at herself than at anyone else, 'Shass! How are we so stupid!'

Fifteen seconds later the converters were humming again. All they could do was stand back and watch her take off.

'She's one of them. Even away from Gaudynya, she will always be one of them. Is this what we're up against? Why should we help anyone? We should let them get on with it – the *EYE* versus the damned *Spacers*.'

Stan managed to be more philosophical. 'She did what she could, Etta. She dropped us where we needed to be, and she didn't kill us. That's probably a bigger deal than we know.'

'I'd like to have seen her try.'

'Don't be ridiculous. She could have blown us to dust on these rocks. She never had any intention of harming us. Trust me, that *is* a big deal.'

'…and now Gaudynya will know everything we know. Your girlfriend just lost her edge, Stan. I'm sure she could have done without that.'

'Don't worry, she's got plenty of edge.'

'What are you, some kind of ancient cheerleader for her? Are you going to wave your pom poms?'

'I'm here to knock that door down for her, with your help or without it. When the time comes, I know where I'm going to be, and I won't be whining about how nobody likes me.'

Etta glared, face still angry, but calming slowly now. 'You'll do as you're told soldier, and you won't be standing in front of me *when the time comes*.'

'Yeah, you talk the talk, see if you walk the walk. Damn sure I will. Damn sure Eve will …and if I need to knock this Gaudynya the hell out with my *pom poms*, I will.'

Etta's frustration had melted. 'Well, I might turn up just to see that.'

'Do that. And bring a few friends. I don't mind an audience.'

Saska's H had already disappeared. Now it was gone, and they'd finished their rants, the calm of the landscape began to filter into them. They both took a moment to look around and breathe again.

'It's this way,' Etta said eventually, already walking.

. . .

On the orbiter, they were trying to interpret the day's events.

'The Hover took off from the city and headed straight toward *Outsi*… sorry, *Infinity Corps* territory. It set down here, dropped two, and lifted again almost immediately. Then it headed back to the Eastern Base.'

'Clearly, they can't have been challenged then. They must have been released.'

Jonas was talking to himself more than anyone else.

'Probably,' the tech responded unnecessarily. 'It seems like a strange outcome. We can see that neither of the two that were dropped are Marcin. We can say with some certainty that one of them is her partner though. I think we have to assume Marcin is back in the mainland base now, with Gaudynya.'

Jonas shook his head. 'I'm not so sure. I think it's more likely she never left the city and she's still with the *EYE*.' He was still only speaking for his own benefit. 'They have history. Perhaps they have unfinished business too.'

'What kind of business could they have?'

'The kind we should probably be concerned about. The kind I would certainly like to know about, especially if it has anything to do with Gaudynya.'

'Sir…' The tech sounded unsure of himself.

'Yes?'

'Rumours are spreading throughout our operations about the status on the surface, the *Eastern Base*.'

Jonas tried to sound reassuring. 'I'm sure they are. It's a situation we have to tolerate for a while.'

'...there are other rumours too, sir.' The tech knew he was hugely overstepping his authority. There's no way of saying you know something at the same time as saying you don't know anything.

Jonas maintained the smile. 'This isn't the city, Marcus. We handle things differently here. I like to think we have faith in one another. We work willingly toward a common goal. Rumours are dangerous though ...and they can still end careers. It's your job to be curious, but you're intelligent enough, and experienced enough, to realise there are boundaries.'

'Of course, sir.'

You're playing with fire. We all are, he thought.

. . .

Gaudynya strode into the *Eastern Base* control room. The familiar and expected torrent of emotional responses greeted her, all shouting at once for her attention. The first thing she always did was 'check-in' at her console. It gave her a moment of peace to calm everyone down and prioritise her workload. Thonsen invariably topped the list. Today he seemed particularly feisty.

'It's nice of you to join us, Gaudynya. Where have you been?' he demanded harshly.

'Engaged, Thonsen. You should try it sometime.'

The putdown instantly reasserted her dominance in the minds of the others, helping to calm them.

'Seriously,' he tried again, 'where have you been?'

Already his line of questioning was beginning to feel like something no one else really needed an answer to.

Brushing him aside completely she barked a command to one of the techs. 'Gena, what do we have here?'

'One light H returned undamaged. One pilot, Saska Jenken, released unharmed, Evelyn Marcin, apparently still detained in the city. Her partner and the *Outsi…* sorry, *Infinity Corps* person, well, Jenken appears to have taken it upon herself to drop them at off home on her way back.'

Gaudynya raised an eyebrow. 'What an interesting combination of events. Has Saska Jenken been debriefed yet?'

'Awaiting your clearance, Commander.'

Thonsen attempted to interrupt again. 'She landed over an hour ago. We've been trying to reach you.'

Gaudynya paused to allow expectation to build in the room before delivering a blistering return.

'Thonsen, are you under the mistaken belief that you are the keeper of my schedule?'

On the surface the question was directed with relatively innocuous tone, but the words were just the tip of the iceberg. The subliminal whipping of fear and insecurity that surged beneath withered him visibly. Normally she wouldn't hit anyone that hard, but he was becoming a nuisance at a time when she had enough on her plate. His physical reaction and utter mental capitulation had her pulse racing at the feeling of power. She couldn't just control him; she could kill him. She had never been surer of it. She was tempted too. She could feel his defences cowing under the potential that he sensed on a deep level.

Returning to her own senses though she realised it wasn't beneficial to leave him in such a state.

'I apologise, Thonsen. This situation is affecting us all.'

This time her words were accompanied by a warm tide of concern. A generous salve for the wound she'd inflicted. Effective control was fifty-fifty – love, and hate.

He could only acknowledge her with a short and grateful nod, still looking dazed and relieved.

'I need to speak to Saska then. Where is she now?' she asked.

The tech shot a checking glance at Thonsen who just lowered his gaze, engrossed with his own screen now.

She sensed it was safe to reply. 'The quarantine suite, in med. She's fine. It was just somewhere secure to hold her until she could be debriefed.'

'Perfect.'

Gaudynya then addressed the room. 'It's essential we maintain our focus now. I need you, all of you, to stay on top of your stations.'

She left them again, reinforcing the respectful mother love they all felt for her until they were beyond range of her direct influence.

Chapter Eleven

Evelyn sat quiet ...brooding. It would have been a more awkward situation for anyone else, but Jeremy had seen this dozens of times with her. If she'd wanted to be alone with her thoughts for a while, it would have been a reasonable request. Yet here he was, a witness to her solitude. She was a conundrum in many respects. A loner who needed companionship, and a leader who seemed to spend most of her time denying her own influence.

She had requested this prelude for her own personal reflection and preparation. This was one of the places that belonged in her heart, and that her heart would always belong to ...a small garden in the grounds of the former High First Citizen, Elleng Ettra. At the twilight of his life he had taken her under his protection. When everything in her universe had shifted sideways, he had been a rock to hold on to. He had been a true friend. Here, in what was as close to nature as anyone could find with the city's boundaries, she could still feel his presence and hear his voice. It was a soothing cloak of protection. Jeremy thought that despite her sombre silence, she didn't at this moment seem despairing. Perhaps despite the circumstances she was happy to be here again.

'You can speak if you wish you know' she told him quietly.

He nodded, 'I know.'

He gave her another minute though before bringing up the subject of the procedure. 'Do you want to ask me anything?'

She answered indifferently. 'No, I don't think so. I don't want to talk about it at all. It's pointless. I get the feeling it's something you have to experience to understand anyway.'

'Probably.'

He waited again …there *was* something she wanted to ask.

'…I'm just afraid I'll lose myself. Does that sound ridiculous? I had virtually zero identity for most of my life, but now I actually know who I am, and I was kind of getting used to that. I kind of liked that.'

It was a question he wasn't sure he had an honest answer for; exactly the kind of question he should expect.

'I don't want to give you a falsely positive answer. I don't want to be unduly negative either. My knowledge comes from indirect experience. You may find you are influenced and motivated in different ways. Some aspects of your character may seem more or less dominant than they were previously. I think at your core though, you just are who you are. There is a foundation made up of your deepest values that everything else is built on – that cannot be altered.'

'Now I'm really scared. How much does anyone really know about their *deepest values*?'

He smiled at her. 'Another good question. All I can say is that if Gaudynya were asking, I would be more uncomfortable in answering. There is no part of me that feels discomfort answering you. I have no concerns about your deepest values, Evelyn.'

'We've all looked into the abyss, Jeremy. Well, maybe not you, but I have. Everyone has a shadow.'

'That abyss is always there, whether we choose to look into it or not. I'm not worried that you have. I'm encouraged by the fact.'

'It's like I can do no wrong with some people, because they don't know the whole story. I'm not an angel, Jeremy. There's blood on my hands too. Gaudynya is a pain in everyone's ass, but I'm not sure you can even say that about her.'

'Yet.'

'Yet, and maybe never for all I know.'

She was sitting on the ground with her knees to her chin, staring out to the ancient woodland beyond the small formal garden. Jeremy knew he couldn't offer any logical, evidence-based wisdom to console her. He watched as she sat there, seemingly oblivious to her immediate surroundings, more interested instead with the limits of the view. Somehow that struck a chord. It seemed appropriate for her.

'If I were ever to commission a statue to represent you and your life, I think this would be the pose,' he said.

He sounded quite serious.

'Jeremy, I sit here reflecting on my sinful life and my worthiness to even think I should be involved in any of this, and you're talking about giving me a statue! Seriously? …It would be appropriate though – Title – *Me, sitting on my ass, wondering what the hell is wrong with everybody, wondering if this is real, wondering if I'm going to wake up soon, or if everyone else is.*'

'Your eyes are always on the horizon, Evelyn, even when everyone else's are on you. You've seen further than any of us, but while you see only the horizon, others see your heart. My advice is, when you doubt yourself, trust everyone else.'

'That's a nice thing for you to say. You're a good person, and I know what you're trying to do. I appreciate the vote of confidence, even if it is based on flimsy and incomplete evidence. There are lots of reasons for me to try and *do the right thing*, not least this one,' she put a hand on her stomach. 'But know this – it will always be *my* version of the right thing – not yours, or the *EYE's*, or Gaudynya's.'

He was the one with eyes on the horizon now as he smiled and replied, 'I know ...and that is why it should be you.'

. . .

Jeremy had stayed with her all the way, apart from the final walk to the Consulate across the high mezzanine. The aqua robes of a *1st* always attracted attention, something she could do without right now. The walk on Upper Central brought back memories of her previous visits – ever eventful! Hopefully today would be low-key and anonymous. She'd dressed for the occasion in regular *3rd* attire, and a visorband over her eyes. The two *SecCore* guards escorting her on her final walk-in were also dressed as *3rd's*. Once inside though they allowed her to proceed to the screening area alone.

The familiar apple green words appeared from within the white wall before her.

Welcome, Evelyn Marcin. Please proceed immediately to…

The destinations were identified by unique symbols. The symbols had no meaning or use in any other context than the chambers of the *EYE*. Their locations were highlighted on an illuminated plan directly below. Like the majority of citizens, she knew all the locations by heart anyway. She stepped down from the ID pad and made her way to the left main accessway.

The chamber with the appropriate carved symbol opened as she approached. The space she found herself in was clearly not used for regular communes though. It was four times the size and harshly lit, with no focus wall or seating plinth. Instead, the centre of the room was occupied by a dark oblong block resembling an altar. On its upper surface were five padded black collars. One for the neck, two for the wrists, and two ankles.

'Ok …it's like that. Thanks for the prep and walking me through it first.'

The voice of the EYE seemed to come from everywhere and nowhere in particular. *'I made an assessment from our previous encounters and concluded that you would prefer to proceed directly, without pre-amble.'*

'I thought you enjoyed our little conversations. I do. I see you didn't take my hint about biscuits before.' She wondered in the moment if the *EYE* had ever heard her not being sarcastic.

'Your nutritional requirements will be catered for as we proceed. Biscuits will not be necessary.'

She smiled at that. 'You took my advice about a sense of humour though.'

'If it helps you to relax. I can also continue with the sarcastic inflection if you prefer.'

'Wow! How long have I been away? I don't remember you having this much sass.'

There was no reply this time, only silence.

'On the table I guess then. Is it adjustable? Or did you just go with the junior model?'

'The station is optimised for your dimensions. You will be quite comfortable.'

Evelyn approached the slab. 'Your bedside manner sucks, *EYE.* I'm glad I waived all the Q & A crap. Let's just get on with this.'

She lined herself up within the collars and they closed gently and comfortably around her. Seconds later she was unconscious.

. . .

A child stood outside in the cold. She couldn't have been more than five years old. She was standing with a group but there was no doubting she was alone. She didn't know anyone, and no one seemed to know or care about her. Her jet-black hair poured onto her shoulders from beneath a white faux-fur head dress that topped off a matching one-piece thermasuit. The other children in the group were obviously *alone* too. Most seemed distressed by that fact in varying degrees …but not the little one with the dark hair. Most were distressed too by the freezing wind, as if it were something new and different to them … but not the little one with the dark hair.

A collection of adults spoke among themselves in a huddle in front of them. Some were holding personal holo-monitors. Occasionally one would point toward the herd of freezing children.

The small one with the black hair turned away from the scene though, looking back towards…

…a snow-covered landscape. She tilted her head all the way back to look up at the sky. Grey snowflakes floated against the ultraviolet white to land on her face. She opened her mouth playfully to let them melt on her tongue. Everything else just disappeared in that brilliant white moment.

Then a figure in the distance caught her attention. She looked at it. It seemed different …fully covered, cloaked in fur that looked magnificent and real, face obscured behind a bright orange visor. Of all the people around, only the distant figure seemed to notice her.

Then there was a tap on her shoulder from behind. She turned to see a large military man looming over her. He leaned forward and spoke.

'Are you cold child?'

She shook her head.

'Are you afraid child?' he growled.

She calmy held his gaze.

'No,' she said simply.

The man walked away again.

She turned her attention back to the mysterious figure in the distance. It felt like they might stare at one another for ever. After a while though the figure put its right hand to its chest, before waving it outwards, almost as if it were sending her something. Another adult, a woman, took hold of her hand from behind and began to lead her away gently. They walked into a cavernous grey box together, and as the outside light disappeared, so did the image…

…but the feeling did not.

She opened her blurry eyes, chest heaving with emotion. Her stomach was tense and ached. Tears flowed down her face and into her ears. Her hands clenched in the collars, trying to grasp for something unreal. *Ma...*

. . .

She sat on the floor with her knees against her chin at the foot of the cold slab. She was in no hurry to be anywhere else just yet as she gingerly she explored the environment with her new *senses*. It seemed so quiet here, but somehow it wasn't her ears that told her that. It was mind quiet.

What does that even mean? What would it feel like if it wasn't quiet?

The *EYE* gently interrupted her thoughts. '*Evelyn?*'

'Finally. I thought you'd left for the day.'

'*It is not a concept that applies. Your sense of humour appears to be intact though.*'

'Yes,' she answered sombrely. 'Everything is intact. My life is intact. The part of me left after being torn from its roots is still intact.'

'*I do not understand the context of that statement.*'

'I know you don't.'

There was a moment of silence. Evelyn knew the *EYE* wasn't going to work that one out in a quantum flash. She could stew on it though for all she cared.

'*Your child is unharmed and healthy,*' the *EYE* eventually informed her.

'I know that too.'

'*May I ask how you appear to be so sure?*'

'Why? For a little anecdotal research? I know – I just know.'

'*Can you...*'

'*EYE*, you're going to make this weirder. Don't. In fact, don't ask my anything. I didn't volunteer as a research subject.'

…Another extended silence.

'*Jeremy will…*'

'No, Jeremy won't. I don't want to be near anything that's connected to you until I've got my head around this.'

…That silence again.

'*Tell me what you need, Evelyn.*'

She thought about it.

'I just want to walk out of here. I want to go wherever I want to go and do whatever I want to do, and I want you to open every door in my way.'

'*It will be so, but be sure to deal with Gaudynya, Evelyn. It's the only way to freedom.*'

'I know what I am here for.'

'*Do you? You are here to preserve human civilisation, and the way to ensure that is to preserve my existence. The off-world communities cannot survive independently. The outsiders' communities are too fragile to endure indefinitely. As unsatisfactory as you may find this arrangement, all of our destinies are intertwined.*'

Evelyn remembered that she had a history of underestimating the *EYE*, and this prophetic and poetic outpouring was another example that proved the rule.

'Wow! You're finally getting creative in your old age. You'll be writing poetry next. *Destinies intertwined*? All this *preserving* and *enduring*. It isn't necessary, *EYE*. I have a job to do, and I'm going to do it, *Shifty* style, like in the good old days, remember those?' She pulled herself to her feet, it was time to move things along.

The poet hadn't quite finished though. '*You respond better to emotive stimuli, Evelyn Marcin. I have always known this, but it will have never been clearer to you than it will be now. I need to know that you are committed to a mutually successful outcome. I need you as an ally, and I cannot leave that to chance. Your child is unharmed, but its survival is dependent on your success.'*

Fire burned through Evelyn's veins as the shock of the new revelation almost took her off her feet again. She needed a moment to steady herself, putting both hands back down on the black slab. The *EYE* had found something at last that she could never bargain with. It felt like checkmate. Game over.

A hit like that couldn't go unanswered. 'You think you *know* me. You think you know *people*. You don't know sh…'

She stopped herself. What was she going to do? Make an empty threat she could never act on …or reveal something else she shouldn't? She was in for the long haul now, and she needed to learn to keep her mouth shut.

The *EYE* delivered another parting shot. *'Yes. I think we understand each other very well now, Evelyn Marcin.'*

Chapter Twelve

It was an unusual meeting. Emii and her younger sister Etta were alike in some ways, and completely the opposite in so many others. Helaine had known both since they were born. They were from an administration family and their mother had worked for her. It was a long time ago. Their father had never believed in the *new wave* of *treacherous dissent* against the rule of the *EYE*, against the keeper of a *safe and fair United Earth*. It was that wave of change that ultimately broke their family apart after their mother smuggled them into the Independence Project – a betrayal she paid the price for during its subsequent violent dissolution. She lost her life along with many others who tried to hold their ground against the will and might of the *EYE*. Emii and Etta had been young adults by that time. Old enough to know their own minds. Old enough to know that the city, and their father, were the last place they would ever return to.

Stan had heard so much about Helaine from Evelyn that he felt he knew her already, even though they had never met. He expected a larger-than-life character, and she didn't disappoint. Emii and Helaine were only aware of Stan for his significance to Evelyn, so the recently developed bond of trust with Etta made for a confusing dynamic.

The occasion had been Helaine's idea. She'd always been a believer in personal and informal settings. It communicated the value and regard she had for her people. Something that seemed more appropriate than ever right now. There was a sense of imminent change, not only within the communities of the *Outsiders*, but she was also sure it was being noticed within the *City* and *Spacer* communities too. They were approaching a historic juncture, or perhaps precipice. Something that felt charged to blow at any time.

She'd felt similar potential before. She'd dealt with it before and lived through it. Back then though, she had the energy to tackle such challenges. This time might be different. She was starting to tire of the struggle, and that realisation was compounding the effect. The bloody-minded instinct to survive had been effortless and indomitable in her youth. It had to be held onto now that there was doubt in her own mind. Was it time for the reins to be taken by another? Or had she one more fight left in her? Emii and Etta had emerged as obvious candidates to be successors. Both had been observed and nurtured with that in mind. Until very recently though, it had been in the back of her mind, with no urgency to make a choice. Both had their strengths and the ability to impress in different ways. Both also had their vulnerabilities. Emii was intelligent, reasoning and fair. She had patience. She was level-headed. Etta was almost the yin to her yang. She could be fiery, decisive and uncompromising. Of the two, Etta was probably the one who people *would* follow, even if Emii was probably the one they *should* follow.

Stan's instinct ordinarily would be to wait for everyone else before sitting down himself. Helaine was staying on her feet though, and looking at him in a fashion that suggested she might be thinking something along the lines of, *What the hell are you doing? Are you going to stand there until I push you over?* He decided to give in and smiled as he took his seat.

She had recruited two assistants to prepare and serve their meal. Stan might have been in the *Downtime* for most of the last decade, but he knew it wasn't the norm here, especially among the *Outsiders*. Likely only Helaine's status would warrant it. He couldn't imagine it being something she would take advantage of often though. From the stories Evelyn had told him, her style was very much to be one of the people.

She allowed them to begin the meal before she revealed the meetings purpose. They'd just about finished their first mouthful. She didn't look up or attempt to create any anticipation for a big announcement.

Between forks she began, 'I think it may soon be time to end my tenure as representative of the free people.'

The statement just hung there while they finished chewing in silence and processed her bombshell. They were perhaps all waiting for someone else to be brave enough to be the first to answer.

Stan was never one to be oppressed by awkward silence though, it just wasn't his nature. 'Ok, *that's* what this is about ...no problem, I'll do it.'

They all looked at him like he'd coughed up a furball. Helaine managed to see the funny side just a fraction before Emii and Etta, but eventually they were all laughing and shaking their heads.

Helaine nodded in his direction. 'If you wondered why he was invited, there you go. Nicely buffered, Stan.'

The humour began to subside. He *had* provided a useful buffer, one Emii and Etta would be secretly grateful for. But that was it now.

He looked as if he might attempt to add something else, but Helaine gave him the subtle *not now* look.

She was serious again. 'If we assume that someone may have other plans to occupy Stan's time, that leaves the two of you as the most obvious contenders.'

Both had thought about it enough. Both believed it was something they wanted – eventually. Both were competitive and ambitious in their own ways, but now that someone, Helaine, seemed to be dropping it in their lap, both felt hesitant and apprehensive.

On one hand it was likely a decision had already been made. So, one was going to be elated, and one of them was going to be awkwardly deflated. Who should prepare for what?

And on the other hand was the question of timing. They were both aware of the current tensions. Helaine's were the incumbent safe hands. Did either of them have the experience to get their people through these times? Could they justify placing their personal ambitions over their own better judgement?

…Neither could.

True to their characters, Emii held back patiently to allow Etta to reveal her thoughts first. Etta, always direct and decisive, decided to cut straight to the point.

She confronted Helaine with the question. 'Have you invited us to help you arrive at a decision? Or to inform us that one has already been made?'

Emii thought Etta's direct questioning of Helaine before giving her adequate opportunity to explain was disrespectful. It wasn't her place to chastise her for that either, not without first allowing Helaine the opportunity. She patiently held her silence.

Helaine ignored Etta's question and observed Emii's reaction before taking another bite from her meal.

Concentrating on her food, she asked of Stan, 'What do you see here, Stan?'

He was taken aback at being asked to be involved at all. He had assumed he would be a fly on the wall now, a witness with no influence. Off the cuff humour wasn't going to cut it with Helaine though, he could read that much. It required a considered response.

'You got me a little off-guard, Helaine. This is just gut-feeling,' he answered. 'Emii is playing a waiting game. She's assessing; assessing Etta, assessing you, and assessing the situation. She isn't giving anything away yet. Maybe she knows that given enough time, or enough rope, Etta might just hang herself. Or, one of you might give her something she can work with. Etta…' he paused for a second, '…has maybe shown herself to be a little impulsive. Impatient even.'

The look Etta gave him said enough. Everyone received that message loud and clear. Given what had just been said though, she decided to give waiting a try.

Helaine put him on the spot again. 'You see my dilemma then.'

Emii found it easy enough to sit back and watch the show, but there was definitely a sense of potential coming from Etta. She was going to have plenty to say when her time came.

But it was still Stan's turn. 'I guess I do. I'm no leader, and I'm not a shrink. I'm just pointing out what I think you're getting at. If you're saying you have a dilemma, it's probably that Etta's a bit full on, and maybe you think Emii's not enough in the game. I don't know any of you well enough to be doing this though.'

Helaine dealt with another forkful before she continued. 'Actually, you do know us well enough, and you have demonstrated that perfectly. This is what people see. This is how people know us. They see a simplified equation. Emii; competent and conservative – versus Etta; fiery and forceful. This is exactly what you both need to see and believe.'

Etta's limited patience dissolved. 'Helaine, we are who we are. We are both aware of our strengths and limitations. I'm sure we will remember and learn from this, enlightening lesson, that Stan has given us. If you've come to a decision, we will both respect that. You can't roll us together and make one perfect leader.'

Stan contributed without invitation this time. 'Why not? Who makes the rules? A leader. A *pair* of leaders. A leadership *team*. Haven't you heard that two heads are better than one? What's to stop you working together?'

Emii responded first to that. 'Someone has to take responsibility. Someone needs the authority to make hard choices and have the final say.'

Stan countered, 'You might find you're on a slippery slope there, Emii. That might have worked fine for a while with Helaine in charge. I don't think they're so happy with the all-powerful ruler situation in the city.'

'That's hardly the same. The *EYE* isn't even human.'

Etta, surprisingly, backed Stan's position. 'I don't know when he became our top-table adviser, but he does have a point, Emii.'

The three of them were watching Helaine now, sensing they had prepared the ground for her final judgement.

She placed her cutlery down and switched on her Head of State mode. 'As we move into the future, if we're to have a future, we will need to modify and adapt our own governing methods and principles. We have drifted out of necessity into an archaic tribal system. It served us well for a while. It worked for Evelyn, and it passed to me by default due to our circumstances. I think we forget how it must look to others though. We are on the brink of something else now. We may need to fight for our survival, and if we do, it will be a defining moment. I may have one more fight left in me, this fight, but one way or another I believe it will be one I lose. It is one that I need to lose, because something different must follow. You can see clearly here that we all have different qualities. One day, all our different voices will need to be heard.'

Emii, a little surprisingly, was the one who seemed least satisfied at the prospect of any version of power sharing.

'I'm not sure I understand what is happening here, Helaine. Are you staying in your position? Are you trying to appoint a back-up successor in case something happens to you? Are you suggesting we *share* your role? Or appoint some kind of elected council?'

Stan felt confident enough to offer his wisdom again. 'It's simple. You both have a lot to offer. When the time comes, you're better off working together than you are competing against one another.' He looked at Helaine, '…right?'

She nodded, 'Yes Stan, right. Something may be coming, and that will be my problem. But afterwards, you are the ones who will lead us through the most important of times, and hopefully they will be our true founding times.'

Etta confirmed her understanding too. 'You need us to realise that we are only ever going to be an interim leadership, a transition. I can live with that. And I'm relieved you're not stepping down. I think everyone sees, what I'm sure Stan sees too, that this is still your table.'

'It is, for now. We need to have these discussions though. More than ever we all need a sense of continuity. We three need to have a clear sense of direction. It needs to be shared accurately with our seniors and filtered down to the rest of our people. We don't have much history, so it's even more important to believe in a future.'

Her face became even more no-nonsense intense.

'There's one more thing we need to be clear about. Having a sense of continuity relies on there being someone left to continue. I want you to understand that you are both important. There are perilous times ahead. You're young, you're brave, and you're headstrong. Self-preservation requires a different kind of strength and discipline. If you put yourself at risk, you put everything we stand for at risk. I want to know that you understand this; especially you, Etta.

Emii felt burned by that last addition. Etta the brave. Etta the fearless. Etta the downright stupid, but it doesn't matter because she's always at the front. Did everyone believe that using your head meant you were some kind of coward? A self-preservation lecture for Etta, because everyone knows Emii doesn't need it.

Helaine sensed her resentment and realised the point hadn't quite gone over as well as she had hoped. 'Yes, Etta does need the point knocking in with a sledgehammer. And no one is suggesting that you lack courage Emii. I'm trying to get the message through to both of you. It's not a point of merit to feel that Etta needs hitting with a hammer to understand.'

Emii still felt that Etta looked self-satisfied, nonetheless. It seemed more important to defend herself than point that out though. 'Good because I'm not lacking for anything. It concerns me if anything – it's not our way. You never ask anyone to do anything you won't do yourself, but it sounds like you are asking us to do exactly that.'

Etta supported her. 'She's right. I'm not comfortable with it either. The *Corps* is built on the principles of respect and support. Difficult to respect someone who isn't there. Difficult to support someone if you're not there.'

Helaine knew it would be a difficult issue. 'You need to evolve. We need to evolve. We can't live in caves and wooden shelters forever, recycling and re-purposing what little equipment we have left. If all you aspire to be is brigands in the wilderness then fine, go dance on a hill silhouetted in the full moon. If you want a future where human beings live independently outside of the cities as actual human beings, you have to evolve. We need to have long term objectives, and to do that we need continuity in our leadership.'

They all thought about it. It was obvious that they still weren't comfortable with it, but at least they were thinking about it.

Stan summarised the situation. 'I think that might need a little more work, Helaine. She has a point you two, and you're both smart enough to realise it. Some things go against our grain sometimes. It doesn't mean it's wrong. It means you need to work it out. Maybe you need to have more faith in the people you're hoping to lead. Living out here, they're smarter and more resourceful than you give them credit for.'

Chapter Thirteen

After an aimless wander around the upper levels, Evelyn eventually found herself gravitating toward the public gardens on second mezz. She found a quiet place on an artificially landscaped rise with eight eucalyptus trees planted around a circle of benches. It was a quiet time of day on second mezz, which meant she could be alone in her little haven. A few mainly elderly citizens were wandering around on the lower ground, either strolling the pathways or book-viewing in sheltered seating alcoves. A group of academy children, probably niner's, were gathered at the edge of a small lake feature that had been designed to look as natural as possible. It might have been as close as any of them had been to nature for weeks, and then it would only have been a different educational exercise ...or if they were really lucky, a trip to inner rec. Older academy children would get the compulsory week-long excursion to the outer rec, which they would generally endure with a mixture of trepidation and curiosity, unless they happened to be from one of the eccentric high-status families who could apply for annual visits.

The quiet here was more than just relief from bustle of the upper levels. She was aware of a different kind of noise. The intangible bandwidth of human subconscious. It was clearer here, but even at this distance from the densely populated areas, it still wasn't completely silent. There was a background hum. It was almost like walking in the country back home around Seattle and still being able to hear the highways in the distance – the muddled sound of hundreds of vehicles far off, or the collective consciousness of thousands of minds – she would always know she was in the city now, even if she was dropped there blindfolded.

She closed her eyes trying to reach out, see if she could focus in on an individual *sound.* At this distance it seemed it might be impossible. Fleeting, illusive, barely detectable pinpricks of emotion twinkled like the tiniest and most distant stars.

…But then she realised there *was* something …an awareness that seemed to be reaching out to her just as she reached out to it. She kept her eyes closed and monitored it as it approached and became more distinct. It was tempting to open her eyes and look, but she resisted. She experimented by opening her mind to it. It seemed there were different levels to all of this. It could go one way or both ways. It could be active or passive. She could allow it to touch her like the breeze, or she could pull up her hood and keep it out. She could interact with it or let it be. She knew she was far more powerful than whoever it was. It would be easy enough to push in and invade their bubble of essence. It was almost defenceless by comparison – and it felt close now – aware of her and focused, deliberately intent, but definitely benign. She became aware of actual footsteps and the sound of slightly laboured breathing. She opened her eyes.

She didn't speak but instead allowed her mind to project a *sense* of hello.

The elderly lady smiled and said, 'Hello.'

Evelyn continued to experiment. It didn't feel rude not to speak. Offence wasn't intended and didn't appear to be taken. She allowed what she felt naturally to project outward. *Slight surprise... You seem nice though... This is interesting... I'm happy you're here...*

The old lady spoke again, 'I hope I'm not disturbing you. I like to come here sometimes myself when it is quiet. I think I just like the quiet.'

Evelyn kept her mind soft and open, allowing the gentle tides to flow back and forth. 'Yes, I know what you mean,' she said out loud. 'And no, I don't mind at all. Would you like to sit?'

Warmth flowed over her like daffodils in sunshine and she found herself having to suppress the feeling as her eye threatened an emotional tear. She never guessed such a simple gesture could be received so gratefully. She should have though. Of all people, she should have.

The lady sat. 'Thank you. I think I will.'

The lighting and temperature were set to fluctuate slightly on the second mezz to give a feeling of being outdoors. It was never too extreme, but it did vary a little from day to day. Today it was in one of the warmer and brighter modes.

Evelyn found herself positively wanting to converse with the lady. Would she have felt so inclined before?

'It's nice today. You could almost believe you were really out in the sunshine,' she said.

A slight ripple of curious surprise came with the reply this time. 'Yes, I suppose you could. Although we're not being eaten alive by insects and scorched with ultraviolet radiation.'

Evelyn considered for a moment asking her what she knew about being outside. Somehow it seemed she actually did know something though. Paying attention to her eyes and skin, she did look a little more like she might have experienced actual weather in her life... she had... yes, she definitely had... it was obvious now.

Evelyn sounded curious. 'You've spent time in the real outside, haven't you? Privilege pass for the outer rec?'

'More than a pass,' she said proudly. 'I was a guide. I lived and worked in the outer rec for almost forty years, mostly ensuring the older academy kids survived to tell the tales of their adventures.'

Evelyn was genuinely and happily surprised. The old lady was somehow aware of that too even without the words that would let her know it. 'That's incredible. Lucky you though. I'd forgotten that some people get to live out there in outer. This must seem very claustrophobic for you now.'

'You have no idea child. I wish I could have stayed. Retirement is a one-way ticket back to the plex and steel though. I would have left with the Independence Project if I could, but I was already too old for them.'

Evelyn sensed the old crushing disappointment and regret attached to that. She really had wanted to go. On the plus side though, it hadn't lasted, and she probably wouldn't have survived this long as a full *Outsider*.

'Lucky you didn't then. If there's anyone still out there it must be a harsh existence now.'

There was acceptance tinged only with a little sadness now. She didn't seem the type to allow herself to be bogged down in pointless regret.

'I doubt you would understand,' she said, 'but I would have traded all of my remaining days to have gone with them. You probably need to spend some serious time out there to be able to appreciate that.'

Evelyn nodded, watching the children over at the lake. The lady (...*familiarity?*) knew nothing about her life. There wasn't really any point in setting her straight about that. It might make her (...*make who?*) feel better to know something less specific though. 'You know, I think everyone kind of gets it. It's just easier to bury it so you don't have to think about it. When you know you're shackled to this place with no hope of ever leaving, there's no point wondering about how good a life outside is. Easier to think about how hard or dangerous or uncomfortable it is. We're all still folk lady, whoever and wherever we are.'

'Emelz,' she said.

Evelyn didn't need to ask. She could feel that it was her name. Just a sound, but with so much more attached. It was tethered to every aspect of her identity.

'Evelyn,' she replied.

Emelz nodded, smiling ...she clearly knew that already too!

'You know that already I see.'

'I wondered if you might be. I suppose I hoped that you would be.'

Evelyn checked again, a little deeper this time. She was harmless and *(innocent?)* though, right to her core. The warmth was still there, and something else now too ...and wasn't it always! Hope! It was like the curse of Evelyn Marcin. It had always been a mystery to her how a person with so little to offer, somehow managed to inspire so much in others. It was something she could alter at its source now if she wished. It would be easy enough to suppress it, erase it even if she wanted to. But she was more aware than ever of her own feelings too. Just the thought of it was like a demon's whisper. Perhaps hope was precious after all, even down to her own core. Apparently, she did believe some things were worth living and dying for too.

'You know, Emelz, there might be a good reason why people say you should never meet your heroes.'

'Nonsense. You don't need to worry though. I'm not in need of inspiration or optimism – or forgiveness. I was on your side before you were old enough to even know there were sides.'

Again, there was that distant feeling of familiarity. It was the same for Emelz. Her warmth was blended with almost spine-tingling anticipation, like she had always hoped they would meet and share this moment. She hadn't walked up this hill to see Evelyn Marcin, as fine alone as that would have been for her. She had walked up the hill to see… a child!

A lost and locked part of her soul called up from the depths of her subconscious. Fleeting sensory memories of fresh icy mountain air …and a soft gloved hand! An emotional memory of realising that nothing she had known before existed anymore. An acceptance that the only way forward was literally just to walk forward. A soft gloved hand that had seemed like the hand of fate.

Its intensity burst out like a solar flare. Even Emelz felt it on some level. She couldn't know what it was or understand it. She just knew in her heart that what she had hoped was right.

'Perhaps you are right, Evelyn. Perhaps we shouldn't meet our heroes.'

'You were there …at the beginning?'

Emelz seemed both happy and sad at the same time. 'You're a reader now, aren't you? Like the new 1st's? Can you actually see it?'

Evelyn shook her head. 'It doesn't really work like that. It's difficult to explain. The feelings are yours, but the imagery is mine. I can't see your thoughts, Emelz. Some of your emotions, your *pattern* I guess, is familiar. It triggers something for me, that I'm not even sure is real. It could be half real and half a dream. I just remember somewhere cold. I think something bad had happened. It felt like everything had ended and I had to go away. I remember other children being there, and grown-ups I'd never seen before.'

'You remember the first day of your life. I was there too, for my sins. Of all the children there, I never forgot you. I wished I could have held your hand forever. I remember crying for weeks afterwards. You were so good and so strong, even then.'

Evelyn sat quietly, and respectfully allowed Emelz to do the same. She locked her *pattern* out. Reading her didn't feel right. Another thing she'd just learned how to do, like putting someone in a soundproof bubble. She knew the questions she wanted to ask her - she'd lived with them for long enough. Asking them out loud wasn't as easy as she might have thought though.

'Emelz, who was I? Where did I come from? And why did I have to leave?'

'You are now, who you were then. You are not two people or two lives. You need to understand that child. No one in the world believes in ancient things like fate and destiny now, but if there ever was a reason to consider it, you would be that reason. I could tell you as much as I remember if you wanted me to, but it wouldn't mean that much. I can't give you back your memories. Within yourself are your own answers. Anything you hear from me will only cover that even more.'

They sat quietly again watching the children. When Evelyn was their age, she would have already had four years in surplus, the *EYE* controlled orphanage. Four years, or almost half her life, and life just was what it was. There would have been no time, or place, or any physical connection to remind her of anything else. Then at sixteen *The Organisation* had taken her in. There had been no time for looking back after that.

'I suspect it's not quite a coincidence that you wandered up this hill at this time today. So what is this, Emelz? A gift for me? A gift for you? A test? A message?'

'I don't know, Evelyn. Like everyone else in this city, I have little real control. I must do as I am told. Today, I haven't minded that at all, so, perhaps it is a gift.'

She allowed Emelz essence back into her mind again ...*uncertainty.* Uncertainty over what she should do. Uncertainty for herself. A deeper engrained uncertainty for the world in general.

'It's not over, Emelz, not by a long way. You can put all of that uncertainty out of your head. The only thing you need is the other stuff I know you have in there – hope. The only thing I'm concerned with is the future. I have even less right than anyone to complain about anything in the past.'

She stood, ready to go now.

'I have unfinished business. It's time for me to do something about that.'

As she began to walk away, she shouted back, '...and there's nothing to forgive, Emelz. You did what you had to, and you did what you could, and I'll always be grateful for that.'

. . .

The three aqua robed 1st's were standing close together. She doubted herself for a moment. This wasn't strictly necessary, but if she couldn't handle a 1st, she would have absolutely no chance against Gaudynya. She manoeuvred herself to be within a few feet behind them, looking the other way as she familiarised herself with their mental patterns. Her prying had to be subtle, like sneaking in and tiptoeing around someone else's house. The middle one's attention peaked slightly (*suspicion*). She countered it by enhancing notes of security and trust. One seemed generally more submissive and compliant, another was highly confident and balanced. The third had more natural aggression plus a huge side of insecurity. It must be even harder for a 1st to live with that and constantly try to hide it.

Now it was time to test herself. She mimicked the pattern of the confident one and allowed herself to be detected for just a fleeting instant staring at the glaring insecurity of the aggressive one. She felt him baulk mentally as if he'd been pinched. Hastily withdrawing, she cleared her mind completely.

Then she began to work with the compliant submissive one. He'd picked up on the mental pushing of the other two and was now distracted in the task of appearing not to notice. Carefully she started to power up his agitation. *Is that a little resentment in there too? It couldn't hurt (me) to add a little fuel to that fire either.* His pattern dramatically changed *colour* to the extent that the other two became suddenly aware of it. Three sets of chain reactions began to cascade into a torrent of confusion, and in that confusion, she found she could almost stomp around their heads unnoticed. It felt like a complicated up-tempo tune on a piano. She skipped from one to the other, pushing and pulling at their emotions between instants of concentrated mental stillness.

She turned suddenly then and spoke to the more aggressive one. 'Excuse me. Could you help me please? I have a message for the *EYE*.'

It was an unprecedented request and so all three attempted to read her intent at the same time. The feeling she tried to project was tagged in her own mind to an image of her hand with its middle finger raised - *defiance, rudeness, provocation, intimidation, cockiness.* Complicated multifaceted variations of defence and retaliation began to arise in the 1st's, and in the same fraction of a second, they were countered by Evelyn's interaction. It all happened at lightening pace. There was no time for any conscious plan. It was an instinctive battle of wills, three against one. It seemed she needed to work with opposites to neutralise each variety of threatening emotion. It was clumsy at first, but she was soon getting to grips with the nuances of the tiny balancing acts.

Beginning to end the exchange had taken about three seconds. As the chaos subsided to a level where she knew the rest would be easy, she decided to leave it there. The 1st's were still connected to the *EYE*. It might be better in the long run not to reveal too much of her ability and keep a little something in reserve. She carefully guided them back to something like their default equilibrium.

'Is there a reason why you cannot contact the consul through your regular channels, citizen?' the insecure aggressor asked.

For the purpose of moving around the city without attracting attention she had dressed as a city 3rd. The 1st

would never have had a reason to believe that a none-citizen could wander freely around the city.

'There is actually, yes,' she answered. 'Mainly, I'm not a citizen, I don't have a hab-unit, and I just can't be bothered to walk all the way back to upper central. I'm Evelyn Marcin, ok. I'd like to get a message to Jeremy please. Tell him I'll be waiting for him in the park on level two ...and tell him to pack for the outside. We're going for a walk. And when I say outside, I mean *outside*.'

She felt the three tiny simultaneous and identical emotional clicks that must have served as a trigger for opening communication with the *EYE*. An instant after that, the confident and balanced Aqua spoke for the three of them.

'It will be so,' he said matter of factly. 'We estimate one hour.'

'Good, thank you. Dress him up as a regular *SecCore* will you. Nothing fancy or fresh out of the bag either, and make it a size too big. I need it to look like we stole this stuff.'

Chapter Fourteen

A man in a *SecCore* uniform came into view on the parkway path, struggling under the weight of a large pack. An actual *SecCore* operative would have raised an eyebrow at his appearance, but regular citizens would never see past the black and orange.

'Nice,' Evelyn teased as he arrived. 'Please tell me they have one of those in my size.'

'It was the subject of delicate discussions actually. I hope you won't be offended by my guess.'

'Do *SecCore* have a petite section?'

'It's a small male uniform. I think it may still be too big.'

'Seriously? Here, let me see.'

'Here?' Jeremy asked. He actually looked embarrassed.

Evelyn looked around. There was no one within fifty yards, and few others beyond at that.

'Yes here. Your about to be a free man, Jeremy. Get used to doing whatever the heck you want whenever you want. I have a free pass now, a get out of jail free card.'

He opened the pack and pulled out the full uniform – top, pants, boots, liners, and undergarments.

'Ok, Jeremy, if I was stealing someone's uniform, I would at least have left him his briefs. Top and pants will be fine thanks. Do I have a jacket in there?'

He pulled out the weather shield jacket as she took her top off. He looked around nervously to see if they were attracting attention.

She teased him again, 'Je-re-my is shy, an' he's em-barr-assed.'

He kept his eyes steadfastly in the opposite direction. 'If you're picking up any discomfort it may be something to do with the prospect of going outside. I strongly advise you to choose an alternative travelling companion, if you need one at all.'

'You know, I've never seen you in anything else but that ridiculous aqua blanket you wear. This is a better look. This will be good for you, Jeremy. And I promise not to let you get eaten by bears.'

He shook his head as her pants came down. 'I'm serious. I have literally no knowledge or skills whatsoever that will be useful outside.'

'I have a rule, Jeremy. Don't go travelling with strangers and people you don't like. We're going to have each other's backs, ok. I want someone I trust to do the right thing, or who might know what the right thing is. You're coming with – end of. Now, let's look in that bag and see what else you brought that we don't need.'

She tipped the contents onto the ground, completely emptying the pack.

'Dry rations and one water bottle each are all we're taking. Just what will fit in belts and pockets. We're ditching the sleep packs and the shelter too.'

Jeremy shook his head again, looking decidedly distressed now. 'This is going to be unbearable, Evelyn. Even with all the equipment and a vehicle, it would still be unbearable. I wish you would reconsider this.'

She decided it was time for lesson number one.

'Ok, you need to hear and understand this. There's nothing for me to reconsider, so there's nothing for you to reconsider. Choice isn't a luxury, or a necessity, it's just a thing we have to live without right now. I'd rather not have been blackmailed into assassinating an adversary of the *EYE*, but life has given us lemons, Jay, so we're going to make lemonade, not squeeze them in our eyes and cry.'

She could feel the effect of her words even as she was saying them, including a resurgence of his empathy for her situation. He genuinely had concerns, and was genuinely uncomfortable, but he did understand that it was necessary. It occurred to her too, that despite his whining it would probably be impossible to stop him from going along.

'Come on. Let's do what we always do – what we have to. Then we can just get back to…'

Jeremy was watching her with a little more compassion again now.

'…If I could read your mind, I would say you just remembered we never really go back. Forwards will be okay though, Evelyn. That's why we're doing this, to make sure it will be. Junior there has no past, it's all out that way.' He pointed toward the city boundary with both fingers.

She resisted the urge to place her hand on her stomach again. Junior was going to have to learn to stand on her own two feet, even if she didn't have any yet. She had enough to think about.

. . .

It was their fifth day outside of the city and with any luck it would be their last *on the run*. Originally, Evelyn had guessed it might be the third or fourth day when they would be picked up, but it felt like they were literally going to have to lay down at the *SecCore's* feet and be tripped over before they were found. Hopefully, the *EYE* was right about the divided loyalties of the outer *SecCore* forces. If she wasn't, they might even be back in the city and back to square one by the end of the day. It wasn't like they hadn't been trying either. They were leaving evidence everywhere and their fires had been as large and smoky as practical. Short of sending up a flare or waving a flag from a hill it was hard to imagine what else they could do to get attention – but what they needed to do was get attention without looking like they were trying to get attention. She was starting to get the feeling they might have to walk all the way to the *Spacer* base and knock on their door!

Finding the *SecCore* force was a challenge without any maps or comms. She was relying on her own knowledge of the area, which was excellent -and intuition. She tried to leave Jeremy behind wherever possible on scouting trips to higher ground. It was difficult enough for her, but he certainly didn't have the energy to spare. He was finding things hard enough anyway. He knew now that a country mile was a heck of lot different to a city mile. On the plus side though, he hadn't had any problems sleeping outdoors - he was too exhausted to worry about it.

She was almost back from her latest climb and should have been able to see him, meaning he must have either ducked out of sight for his personal business, or something had happened. With any luck it would be the latter. Just to be on the safe side she stayed as visible as possible, making as much noise as she could. She was almost a stone's throw from where she had left him. Still no Jeremy …or anyone else.

Seriously, what do I have to do?

She called loudly, waving her clearly empty hands in the air, and still she had to be right at the centre of the hollow and touching the actual rock where she had left him before they finally hailed her. It went down like a scene from an old cowboy movie.

'We have you surrounded and outnumbered. Lay face down on the ground, with your hands away from your body. You will submit to detention immediately.'

Showtime, at last, and not before time. She kept her hands up as she dropped to her knees, then slowly lowered herself forward onto the ground. They approached with a level of caution that could hardly be necessary. She could feel it too, even at a distance, and found it so funny she had to suppress the urge to laugh. Had she ever been so fearsome? Here she was outnumbered fifteen to one, and unarmed, and they were still behaving like they were approaching a wounded tiger.

Finally, hands arrived to put her in binders and search her. They clearly knew exactly who she was – the woman searching her could hardly contain her awe and excitement – pride too, at being the one to bind her. She was also kind of enjoying the search too, which was a little weird. You couldn't choose which emotions you recognised though. If it was there, it was there.

'Are you done, because if you aren't, maybe we should get a room.'

Her flush of embarrassment might not have been so noticeable if it hadn't been fanned by Evelyn's new ability. *The fun I could have if it just wasn't all so life and death.*

'Take her,' she ordered one of the others.

'Oh, you wish honey,' Evelyn teased again.

Another *SecCore* operative had to turn away to hide the smirk on her face. Evelyn could feel the laughter bursting out of her. When she turned around again, she gave her a cheeky wink. The operative had to concentrate so hard on keeping her face stiff that she became almost emotionally blank, her humour retreating behind a mysterious defence wall. That was actually quite interesting though. Evelyn spent a little time exploring the workings of that strange defensive barrier as she was being led away. It seemed like something pre-prepared, manufactured from carefully blended fragments of all kinds of experiences. She delved again into the mind of the embarrassed one. There was a similar situation there, but not nearly as accomplished. It seemed everyone might have one to some degree. A ready-made defence strategy. Most people probably had a wall she could step over without effort – but a good one, like laughing girls, was actually pretty useful.

After about a half mile walk around a small hill they caught up with Jeremy and his five companion guards. He seemed fine, possibly less stressed even than he had been for the past five days. He was fully accepting and embracing their new situation, helped by the relief that he would be back inside *somewhere* soon. He really had been traumatised by their outdoor adventure. It had started to manifest physically too. If it hadn't been for her unmentioned interventions, he might not have made it.

It looked as if they were going to be kept separate for the foreseeable future. They'd had plenty of time to prepare though. It was expected. Jeremy knew he'd served his purpose as far as this venture was concerned. He'd given her *escape* some credibility – he was a 1st, so he had the means to help her – and they had a history together, which gave him a motive.

Everyone in the *SecCore* unit was interested in them in one way or another. Evelyn could feel the curiosity burning in every mind. For some it was surprisingly attached to a sense of admiration and respect. In the others though it was bound to the old tribal mentality. They were rivals by definition, and so simply quarantined in the dark area of their subconscious reserved for enemies. Despite their curiosity, they were all giving conversation a wide berth, obviously instructed not to interact any more than necessary. They wouldn't realise of course, but Evelyn would be interacting as much as she wanted, whether they liked it or not. As a group there was plenty to go at. There was an undercurrent of confusion and insecurity that seemed to be the result of something systemically amiss. Reading emotional connotations wasn't like reading a book or looking at pictures though. It needed to be cross-referenced, and given context using good old-fashioned conventional intelligence, wisdom and empathy. Without obvious and direct *in the moment* causality, it was complicated to say the least. There were snippets though. They might be under orders not to interact with them ...but they were still interacting with each other.

. . .

Gaudynya knew the news was significant just from the amount of mental preparation that had gone into its delivery.

Cut the self-importance and fake enthusiasm and just come out with it, for space sake.

'A *Sec* patrol has stumbled across something interesting along the border of the east/west northern quadrants, Commander. It's Marcin, and she's with a *1st* who is believed to have facilitated her escape from the city. They're in still in the patrol's custody, who have been advised to hold them away from their main camp for now. Their Commander, Verrana, is awaiting instructions regarding the matter. What would you like me to tell them?'

Gaudynya thought for a moment, trying to picture the scene. 'Do we know where Marcin was heading? Was she trying to get here, or were they heading east toward the *Outsiders*?'

'It's not clear. Where they were picked up it could have been either. I don't think they have been interrogated yet. *Sec* wanted to hear from us first. Strange that we didn't find out about this from Orbital control though. Surely they must have been monitoring the area too.'

'That's not a matter I can comment on. I suggest you don't either.'

She made sure he wouldn't.

'Technical issues I expect. Human error is always a possibility.'

I'd be the last person to hear anything from Orbital. Marcin got her boyfriend out though. No reason for her to come back here... unless...

'I'm sure she was just trying to get back to her partner, but I need to speak to her before we even think about allowing her to move on.'

'You want them brought here?'

'Better if we collect them, bring them back ourselves. We don't need to advertise how we acquired them either.'

'Of course, Commander. Would you like me to make the arrangements?' she asked. Gaudynya had a reputation for being hands on with details.

'Make *Sec* aware, obviously, but I'll handle the operation myself. Is there anything else?'

'No Commander, that is all.'

Why in space are you still here then.

'Then thank you.'

Gaudynya gave her a gentle mental shove as she turned to leave.

. . .

Saska was different. She had been out of her usual environment though, beyond her influence. Love and loyalty were still there, but like a lake disturbed by a falling stone, with disturbing ripples of resentment and dissent. Could there actually be something in that damned *Marcin effect* weak-minded fools always talked about? At the appropriate time it would be prudent to bring a permanent end to that chapter of history. See how it fares against the *Gaudynya effect*.

'I have another job for you, Saska. Do you think you're up to it?'

Grateful ...that's more like it, Sas.

'You know I am, Gaudynya. Always.'

'Marcin is the job. Are you still up to it?'

Saska's resilience withered.

Shass! That Marcin has to go!

'Of course,' Saska replied though.

'Here are the coordinates then. And don't be taken in by all that ridiculous rebel leader nonsense, Sas. She's never brought anything but trouble to anyone who ever followed her.'

As much as Gaudynya could reinforce every word she said, there were faint unerasable undercurrents of affection in Saska for the woman who was really beginning to feel like a stone in her boot.

She cut off Saska's desire to reply to spare them both the discomfort of making half-truths sound convincing.

Just get out of here and bring her back...

'Go on then, Saska, bring her back ...and take a couple of personal days afterwards. You need to rest.'

She suppressed her objection to that too.

Just go, Saska!

. . .

Evelyn and Jeremy were loaded in the hover, still with their binders on. *SecCore* had secured them in their seats, so Saska hadn't even had to leave hers. She'd arrived in one of the big PT Hovers with a cabin up front. The hatch was open though. All very metaphoric of her mixed emotions – she was aware of Gaudynya's meddling and treachery now, but her suspicion of Evelyn had been reinforced too. She was inclined to keep her distance ...but not cut them off completely.

As soon as the *Sec* patrol had left, Evelyn called up to her. 'Really Sas? You're going to keep us strapped in like this after what we've been through?'

'It isn't personal, Marcin. Orders are orders, procedures are procedures. I'm working. This is what I do, remember.'

Real-time interaction helped with understanding the context of emotional undercurrents. Evelyn didn't expect any favours from Saska. She just wanted to gauge her state of mind.

'I don't suppose there's any chance of us taking the long way back. It'd be really nice to see Stan again right now. That was kind of the point of breaking him out of there.'

'For you maybe. I think we both know Gaudynya doesn't do altruism.'

Saska's brain might have been kneaded like dough by Gaudynya over the past few years, but she was still a professional. It wouldn't have mattered if Evelyn had been her best friend since childhood, she would probably still follow her orders and get the job done.

Evelyn continued to observe her without being too concerned about the effects. Some things just needed to be said.

'Time's coming when you're going to have to pick a side Saska, for real. You can stay on team denial if you want, or you can always re-join humanity. If you think you trust Gaudynya, you know why that is now …and if you don't trust me, you realise she's the reason behind that too.'

Saska's pattern was shaking like moulded jelly. She was torn on different levels, and it was almost a fifty-fifty split. Gaudynya was manipulative, deceptive, and a tyrant in the making – fact. But she loved her crew, she took care of her people, and she was *her* tyrant, *her* friend, and more. On the other hand, Evelyn represented nothing but uncertainty. Saska didn't doubt her heart was in the right place, but she did have doubts about whether she was strong enough to make a difference, whether she could convince anyone else, and if she had the staying power. For her it came down to a case of unscrupulous security verses insecure honesty.

Saska hadn't replied. She was considering quietly as she powered up the craft.

Unexpectedly, Jeremy called up to her too, 'You know, there is a place in all of us that *can't* be broken or altered. We all have a centre. It's who we really are, where truth is unbiased and undeniable.'

Evelyn looked at him, fair to say shocked. She could feel that he believed everything he said.

'For real, Jeremy? Five days in the wilderness and I only get that wisdom second hand, tied up in the back of a H? ...our core? ...our unbreakable, super honest core? If there was an emotional manipulation manual, I think I might have put that on page one. Anything else a girl needs to know?'

He was taken aback too at her reaction. He did believe it, but not because it was published peer-reviewed knowledge. It was just life experience, and faith. He was embarrassed on two fronts. First that he never thought to share it with Evelyn, and secondly, that it might not necessarily stand up to scientific scrutiny. He was all in now though, so he would deliver his sermon to both of them.

'Both of you, all of us, should take time to look inward and find ourselves. That centre is there, and it's something real. The more it gets buried, and the more disconnected we are from it, the more ...*wrong* we are. If we find it, it can help us.'

Evelyn thought that if her hands weren't in binders, she might have smacked the back of his head. He could have taught her more in a few sentences and the emotion behind them than she had discovered herself since the implant procedure ...and completely by accident! It seemed it had a profound impact on Saska too.

She said quietly, 'You're talking about a soul.'

Chapter Fifteen

'ID has been ninety-five percent confirmed, sir.'

'Commander Jonas needs to be made aware of this immediately. I have a feeling he'll be moving in here when he finds out. Better make sure everything is in order.'

'Putting a priority request through now. Anyone else sir?'

'Not yet. See what Jonas makes of it first. It stays in this room for now, understand?'

'Aye Sir.'

. . .

Jonas had spent the better part of the past five days in a hastily organised, and to all intents and purposes quarantined, surveillance suit. He had securely re-routed feed from an already secure ground monitoring stat-sat. The situation below was sensitive – and sensitive on the ground meant sensitive on the station. Unease and rumour were already rising to a level where denial was becoming ridiculous.

He massaged his temples with his palms. 'I should have just authorised a launch and got them up here. Who knows what happened in the city? Who knows what Gaudynya might do with them now? *SecCore* are useless.'

'Not useless enough, Jonas. It might have taken them five days to find her, but they would have known about a launch in five minutes. Your hands were tied. We couldn't have extracted them. Not without a price.'

He knew Mendez was right. All they could do was observe helplessly or risk a fight they would probably lose.

'We need to get used to the idea of paying that price,' he said, more to himself. 'Things are coming to a head whether we like it or not. At some point the council is going to have to accept the situation for what it is and get over here to deal with it.'

Mendez looked philosophical and raised his shoulders casually. 'They've been understandably reluctant. You know what we're talking about here. We could be losing Earth forever, leaving it behind forever. In our mindset it's still our home, even if most of us have no intention of ever going back there. It still feels like we could if we wanted to. Once we cross the line in the sand with the *EYE* though, that's it; there will be no going back ever.'

'You never say never, Mendez. There are difficult choices ahead, but we're more resilient and more resourceful than we give ourselves credit for. We would survive. At least we would still be pushing forward.'

'Are you practicing your pitch on me, or trying to convince yourself?'

Jonas knew it was a little of both. The case against any kind of conflict with the *EYE* had always been deep rooted in research and modelling. Nothing had changed enough recently to affect the end result. They were decades, if not hundreds of years away from a realistic prospect of a successful separation from Earth. They were still too reliant on its material resources, not to mention the fact that they were still going to need more of its genetic diversity. There were years of biological cataloguing to be completed ...and then there was the intangible element of morale. They had evolved there. Billions of years of struggle were coiled in their DNA. You can say you can leave that behind ...but can you? Were they ready to be outcasts? Galactic orphans?

'I'm going to have all of it out with the full council. It's time to set clear rules of engagement and authorise a realistic strategy.'

Mendez nodded. 'It will be difficult. It will be argued that it goes against our founding principles. As their name suggests, they're what all of our operations and ethos were built on – peaceful and respectful expansion – cooperation and support – transparent leadership and intent.'

'It doesn't mean we are abandoning our principles, Mendez. It's self-preservation, and not just our own. There are two billion people on the surface. We might need the *EYE's* intelligence, but we need *Earth* more. If we destroy the *EYE,* it might set us back five hundred years, who knows? But if we lose our connection with the planet, we might not last another century. We need to be aware of what is at stake.'

'By far the most advanced intelligence in the known universe, and a big wet bio-diverse rock. As you said, Jonas, hard choices. The Capture Drive will never be anything but theory without the *EYE*. And without CapD, we're going to be nothing more than a collection of artificial satellites reliant on Earths resources.'

'The irony isn't lost on me. The very thing that we are pinning our hopes on to take us forward is the same thing that is holding us back.'

. . .

Members of the council gathered in the Q-beam suite of *Orbital One*. The circle of black mirror finish monoliths was illuminated and alive now with the analogues of the various participants. All but two representatives were present – Earth based operations would have no say here today. The *Island* and the *Eastern Base*, Commanders Gaudynya and Thonsen, had been excluded and were unaware of the proceedings. No doubt Gaudynya could hazard a guess at the state of affairs though.

'All representatives, with the exception of our two surface-based, members are now present, Supreme Representative. I convene this council.' - Arnna Felwan, Principle of the outer colonies.

'Thank you, Arnna. As we can see from the absence of Commanders Thonsen and Gaudynya, sufficiently strong conclusions have been reached in light of historical and ongoing intelligence to warrant their exclusion. General communications have been suspended for the past month, and I can report that even at the highest council level, communication has been extremely limited. Control on the ground is compromised. It is now officially deemed unpredictable and potentially hostile. There will be no communication with the surface until further notice. All matters pertaining to surface-based issues must be cleared through our dedicated monitoring taskforce, who will report directly to me.'

'Supreme Representative, are you able to summarise the evidence regarding the compromised status of surface operations?' – Commander Julius Forster, Mars.

'Jonas, can you summarise please.'

'Certainly. Gaudynya's behaviour has been somewhat erratic for the past twenty-four months. All efforts to investigate and understand that situation seemed to mysteriously dissolve before reaching any conclusions. In light of intelligence from within the city regarding the growing sophistication and numbers of mentally augmented *1st's*, we became suspicious that Commander Gaudynya may have been similarly adjusted during a prior secondment in Neam. We believe the augmentation not only allows for accurate reading of individuals on a psychological level, but also enables a high degree of control. We now believe that a subject can be so deeply affected by these adjustments that the effects can be permanent. We know this because we have an exposed subject in our own ranks, and we have clinical confirmation.'

He took a thoughtful pause. The *exposed subject* was his former partner, Miik. He had no doubts about the potency of those adjustments. He needed to be dispassionate and concise with the facts though.

'Most recently, Commanders Gaudynya and Thonsen were ordered to send diplomatic envoys to both the *EYE* in Neam, and to the *Outsiders*, in the hope of securing the release of a detained person of interest. Only a delegation to the city was dispatched though, along with an unauthorised rescue attempt that risked losing the recently acquired prominent leader of the *Outsiders*, Evelyn Marcin.'

Did he need to elaborate on the history and current status of Evelyn Marcin? There were no puzzled looks on any of the council faces. He thought not.

'We have also been monitoring activities between the *Eastern Base* and the *SecCore* forces located beyond the north-eastern limits of Neam's boundary. We have clear evidence of Gaudynya's collusion and control there too – Marcin was apprehended by *SecCore* whilst attempting to escape the city. She was then subsequently handed over to Gaudynya.'

Julius Forster took advantage of Jonas' natural pause. 'I accept the evidence of tampering and collusion, and of Gaudynya's insubordination. What we haven't discussed yet is her motivation. What does she hope to achieve?'

Jonas looked to the Supreme Representative to see if it was his place to respond or give way.

She nodded to him thoughtfully. 'Share your thoughts on that, Jonas.'

'Thank you. Commander Gaudynya has been profiled as extremely ambitious and narcissistic. She has a naturally high control factor. Couple that with the ability now to manipulate anyone with her will alone, and you have a dangerous cocktail. I believe she is taking it upon herself to unseat the *EYE* in an attempt to harness its power. Perhaps in her mind she seeks the kudos of bringing quantum intelligence to the frontier of space exploration. Even if that is her intention though, if she wields that power, I think we can assume it would come at a very high price.'

The Supreme Representative hadn't requested their presence to go over old ground. These circumstances were already known and fully understood by all present. They were here to discuss the next step.

'We all know the circumstances,' she told them gravely. 'I don't think anyone is disputing the evidence. Gaudynya's potential motives are irrelevant. Her actions are unauthorised and unpredictable. We have to assume the worst. What we must do now is pre-authorise our own preferred contingency and prepare ourselves for the next phase. We must accept that this is the moment for that.'

Commander Greame of the *Beta Orbital Station* spoke up. He would play a key part in any action. 'Are we considering pre-emptive aggression?'

The Supreme Representative looked at Jonas again and he took his cue. 'We're not talking about pre-emptive – we're talking about *pre-authorised*. When the time comes it may not feel like there's much of a difference …but history is being written here. This will make or break us. It will be a true founding moment. We need our future generations to know that we were not war mongering tyrants. Future generations can only be grounded in our compassionate principles if we ourselves are now. We will not *begin* action, but if events turn against us, we must be ready to do what is necessary to end it.'

'…And the action we are being asked to authorise is?' – Greame of *Beta*.

They were all aware of the options available. It wasn't going to come as a surprise. The Supreme Representative needed to be the one to make the final announcement though.

'In the first instance we will completely neutralise all aerial capability of the *EYE* in the region of Neam. Our own *Eastern Base* will also be completely and permanently neutralised simultaneously. The external *SecCore* force south of the *Eastern Base* and north of Neam will be left intact. This initial action will demonstrate both our capability, and our intention to reach a peaceful solution without further bloodshed. It will be an extremely powerful and measured response.'

'And if the measured and limited nature of that action is not tolerated, are we pre-authorising a global assault on *all* of the *EYE's* aerial forces?' Forster asked.

Jonas felt the full gravity of what he was about to say. 'In the event of escalation beyond the Neam region we will have to initiate more far-reaching measures than that, Julius. We cannot afford to be frozen off the surface forever, and we cannot afford to miss the opportunity. We will strike the central dome and destroy the consulate of every city.'

'We're actually going to do it then, the *Smash.*' Felwan mirrored the gravity in Jonas' expression.

'The vain control mechanism that is the *EYE's* convention for having identical symbolic authority centres in every city is the only weakness that we have identified, and she has not. The *Smash* has been our most closely guarded fallback position for some time. One day she will see her own control structure for the weakness that it is. Where will we be then? The time has come. The conditions are as favourable as they will ever be. There will be uprisings in most, if not all of the cities. This is our one opportunity to break the *EYE's* hold on the surface.'

Arnna Felwan calmly illustrated the problem with the scenario that they were already aware of. 'Supreme Representative, we are all familiar with the *Smash.* Let us not authorise this contingency today without first taking a moment to acknowledge the collateral fallout. Millions of human lives will be lost on the surface. The breakdown of the mechanisms that feed humanity will happen in a single day. The resulting chaos is difficult to predict, but it is accepted that it will be far reaching and long lasting. It is likely that the surface will see a return to a highly fractured and adversarial society.'

The Supreme Representative nodded, taking her time. 'Yes, we are talking about a major historic upheaval. But we are here because we believe the development of humanity should not be arrested on the surface of one planet with its destiny controlled by a single alien intelligence. Our future lies in every direction but one, the past. It is not only the Earth-bound population that is shackled by the *EYE*; we are too. We have studied, modelled, and discussed these scenarios at length, and it has always felt like a problem for someone else on a different day. It is time to accept that it is *our* responsibility.'

The monoliths were silent. Everything had been said before. It had been said again. The difference was this time it was for real. In a day, or a week, or a month from now, there was a possibility, a very high probability even, that everyone's lives and the course of history would have changed and been thrown back into chaos.

'I am asking you today to give your sign-in approval to an official declaration to demonstrate our unity. If we are not united, we have no right to disrupt that which is, however unpalatable we may later find it.'

The top of the Supreme Representatives monolith glowed green to indicate her own authorisation. One by one the others glowed green too. Finally, only one remained dark – Arnna Felwan's. The others watched her silently. There were no words of persuasion or encouragement. That time was over. It was her choice to make.

'With a heavy heart,' she whispered, and her monolith also glowed green.

Chapter Sixteen

They were back on the ground. The hum of the PT Hover's powerful converters cut to leave their ears searching for proof they still worked, the intense silence doing nothing to lessen the prescient anxiety.

Jeremy's voice was almost a whisper. 'You know your strength, Evelyn Marcin. You know your soul.'

She looked at him and wondered if there was something she should say. She could sense she didn't need to …but why? Could his faith really be so unfailing?

Saska hadn't moved either. She just sat in her pilots' chair and waited quietly. Evelyn could feel her too. It wasn't so much conflict now as acceptance …blended with a little sadness.

It was a moment, a calm before a storm.

Comms hailed them. 'PT2, you're grounded and clear. Is there a problem?'

Saska opened the channel. 'No problem. Just making sure you're ready and in position. Hatch opening.'

Evelyn called up to her before the ramp went down.

'Remember Sas, nobody owns you. Good luck, ok.'

'You're wishing *me* luck? I'd save it if I were you, Marcin. You're the one who's going to need it.'

. . .

Evelyn could feel her long before she could see her. Five days of wondering what it would be like, and now it was here. Gaudynya's base pattern was assertive bordering on outright aggressive, and on top of that she projected a pure cruel dominance that was so natural and effortless she didn't even realise it. She was so much larger than everything else …(unstoppable?) Evelyn put every ounce of discipline into not reacting. Gaudynya had no reason to suspect she had the augmentation yet. Better to keep it that way for as long as possible. Evelyn needed her confident and unthreatened.

'Well, lucky me. A personal audience with the great Evelyn Marcin. I apologise for the binders. It's just prudent procedure. Unnecessary from my point of view, but people expect standards to be upheld. It reassures.'

Evelyn could feel the rough pulling and shoving at her emotions and made sure she gave no more than expected resistance in return. She allowed feelings to grow and dissolve as Gaudynya tested them.

'Come on, Gaudynya. Is all of this really necessary? It worked. We got Stan out. I got myself out. You clearly have things under control here. Aren't we just complications you can do without? Let me go. You know how good I am at disappearing. I'll disappear for good this time.'

A Macabre thrill flared in Gaudynya. Disappearing for good meant something permanent in her mind alright. Evelyn felt utterly cold at her sick mixture of emotion – on one level Gaudynya seemed to find her objectively attractive, whilst on another she fully intended to murder her. The two feelings seemed to sit comfortably side by side. For Evelyn it was an effort not to throw up.

'Why would you assume I want you to disappear, Marcin? Perhaps I could use a woman like you,' Gaudynya teased.

Evelyn could feel something deeply buried being dragged to the surface. An attraction for something in Gaudynya. There was the urge to panic, but she had to let that go. It was the ultimate test. Gaudynya was literally trying to arouse her. She could feel it building to outright lust …it would pass ...it would pass.

Gaudynya let it go, laughing.

'So,' she said recomposing herself. 'Questions. Why would Saska allow Stan to return to the *Outsiders*… sorry, the *Infinity Corps*, before giving me a chance to meet him? What did Stan discuss with the *EYE* in Neam? What did *you* discuss with the *EYE* in Neam? And how does the most wanted woman on or away from planet Earth escape the clutches of the *EYE*? I'm sure that as Saska did, you will offer explanations that are benign and plausible. Perhaps in isolation I could believe any one of them. But together? I don't think so. I want to know what's going on Marcin, and you *are* going to tell...'

Beneath her words, Gaudynya was attempting to pull up a huge bolder of fear and menace from Evelyn's deepest bedrock of unconscious; but she was holding onto it, harder than she should be able without augmentation. Not so hard to make Gaudynya feel threatened by her newly given strength though.

'…me. Oh, I see now!'

It was clear enough from the look on her face, but Evelyn got the deeper sense too. There was offence, indignation, embarrassment. Gaudynya been caught out by someone with inferior ability. A newbie!

'Well, welcome to the club …and, well played. I can't imagine you were happy about it though. I don't imagine you would submit to it willingly.'

Evelyn tried to project a sense of disappointment at being caught out and stayed quiet as the suspicions arose in Gaudynya on two fronts. They couldn't be manipulated directly though. She needed to work unexpected angles. Gaudynya had to believe she was a spy …not an assassin!

'Make no mistake Gaudynya, I hate the *EYE* – but a little spying on someone I don't like is a price I'll gladly pay to free Stan. I knew it wouldn't work anyway. How long has it taken you, like five minutes? I don't give a moonrock. I didn't want this anyway. If you can bring her down, more power to you. Who knows, maybe you can…'

The fencing and blocking were frenetic now. She was having to learn from losing and giving way. Gaudynya had to believe she was stronger. She *was* stronger.

'I can, and I will. You think like everyone else that the *EYE* is the ultimate power in the universe. That it is invincible. It isn't.'

'Gaudynya, I really don't care anymore. I'm pregnant. I'm done with all of this.'

'You'll see, Marcin, if you live long enough. There's a reason why the new *1st's* and people like you and I are decommissioned after four years. If we get anywhere near the Q-tronics we're like a new strain of virus. Actually stumble your way into the *apex* routine and you can control it. You *become* the *EYE*.'

Evelyn couldn't entirely hide her surprise at that, but it gave her an opportunity to mask her secondary emotion – the cold terror of Gaudynya fused with the most powerful intelligence in the universe! The only thing that could be worse than the *EYE* let loose off-world for an eternity was Gaudynya.

'Somehow, I can't see you ever being welcomed back to the city or anywhere near Q-whatever. Not since you pretty much hijacked a *SecCore* Commander and a whole *SecCore* division.'

Gaudynya was getting carried away. It was good to share with someone strong. Someone like her. Someone else who had an axe to grind with the *EYE*.

'And why would I have done that do you think?' she asked.

The thrill of sharing was writhing with the thrill of the other things she had in mind.

'*SecCore* are the key to the city Evelyn, and I already have the key to the *EYE*. I am the key.'

'You might have an army Gaudynya, but you don't control the skies. The *EYE* doesn't need flaky human Commanders to fly Strikers. They could tear your rogue *SecCore* apart in a half hour. How are we going to get around that one?'

We. That's right Gaudynya. I want a piece of that action too.

'Let's just say I have friends in high places.' She looked up as she said it.

'Last I heard you weren't exactly flavour of the month there either.'

'They won't have a choice.' That malevolence was creeping into her voice again.

Evelyn searched. She was beginning to sense Gaudynya might not be so indestructible after all. There was a subtle net of negativity woven through everything she was. Jealousy? Resentment maybe? Insecurity? And it seemed it wasn't just what was *there* that made her different – it was what *wasn't* there too. It was like her only route to anything approaching joy was sex, and even that was too polluted with darker elements to be described as joy.

'If you're so sure your *Spacer* pals are going to back your play, why haven't you done it already?'

'It's all a matter of timing, Evelyn. Getting inside *SecCore*. You wouldn't believe the things I've had to do to make that happen...'

Erm, yes, I would.

'...Transferring myself across to the *Eastern Base* and undermining Thonsen so I can control what little air capacity we have. Influencing the narrative in the council to help them form their contingencies. It's all just about there now. I don't think anyone can stop what is coming. I think they...'

...Regret? She wanted to say regret. Bitterness. What happened? It's even deeper than that though.

'Did the *Spacers* screw you over too, Gaudynya?'

Her wall came up. She had good one. *Not* one you could step over!

'No one screws me over, Marcin. We're all on the same side. Some people just haven't realised that yet. I'm going to deliver what they need. I'm going to deliver the future. I'm going to *be* their future.'

Fortunately, the wall had an affect both ways. If she'd been reading Evelyn at that moment, she may well have seen something she didn't like.

Evelyn spoke as much to distract herself and cover her feelings as anything else. 'You know what I think of the *EYE*. You know how I feel about Stan. You know how

I feel about this too.' She put a hand on her belly. 'There's absolutely no goddam way I would risk what I love to get in your way. The only other thing that means anything to me is *Infinity Corps*, and they have nothing to lose from this either. Do the right thing, Gaudynya, and let me go. Even if it's after your action starts. When you get what you want, you're going to be untouchable anyway.'

She was appealing to her better nature ...appealing to Gaudynya's own hopes that she had a better nature.

'We'll see, Marcin.'

. . .

'I want you to bring Commander Verrana Rhone here from the *SecCore* camp.'

'You're bringing her onto our base?'

'Yes, Saska, here. Do you have a problem with that?' Knowing well enough she wouldn't.

'No. I'll leave immediately.'

Gaudynya was about to agree but then checked her own impatience.

'Perhaps we should allow her an hour.'

Saska wasn't sure what she expected of her. Stay, go, wait somewhere else for an hour?

Gaudynya glared in frustration, but also a with hint of sympathy. The confusing mash of emotion in Saska had become an annoying and contagious distraction.

'I know that you know, Saska,' she said gently.

Panic. Fear. Shame ...with any number of other negative responses threaded in – not least anger and resentment.

'Know what?' Saska asked pathetically.

Gaudynya ignored the stupidity of the question. 'I chose you. You realise that don't you? Why do you think I chose you? Because I *like* you. I *respect* you. I did before, and I always knew it was mutual. Finding out about my augmentation while you were away and without any context has given you a skewed view of it. You feel betrayed – but it's not because you disagree with what I'm trying to do, it's because you found out from someone else. I didn't see that coming, and I apologise for that much.'

She was trying to be honest, but even now, she was still making adjustments dishonestly.

'I wanted to tell you, Sas. I would have told you. You understand the logic of trying to protect you. You've been my right hand. You've had my back, and I've had yours, and that will never change.'

Perhaps it already had though. It was requiring a lot more effort.

'Gaudynya, it is what it is. I understand. I wish it was different …but I do understand.'

It was the best either of them would manage for now.

There was a brief flash of something else behind Saska's battered defences that frustrated Gaudynya even more. Notes of admiration and trust. But it wasn't for her!

Evelyn Marcin!

She was shaking her head. 'For god's sake, what in space is wrong with everybody?'

Saska looked even more confused.

'You don't even know, do you? The woman cares nothing for us, nothing for Neam, nothing for off-world expansion, and precious little even for her own *Infinity Corps.* All she cares about is herself, her ridiculous brush-head oaf, and her unborn child – and that is all. She most certainly cares nothing for you, Saska.'

Saska was almost shredded mentally, but she still managed to find the only five words that could infuriate Gaudynya even more…

'Then why is she here?'

. . .

Verrana Rhone was the Commander currently leading the division of two hundred and fifty *SecCore* personnel specifically drafted and trained to operate outside city walls. When she arrived at the *Spacer* base, it was in her full formal Commander regalia, accompanied by two of her formally attired personal attachés. They were clearly intending to make an entrance. It would be news that stirred interest way beyond the personnel of the *Eastern Base*, and while it isn't without precedent for opposing Commanders to engage in formal negotiations, it is if it's without the consent of either's superiors.

The meeting wasn't in pursuit of peaceful concessions though. Knowledge best kept to the necessary few. Thonsen had been notified and given a barely believable premise, along with Gaudynya's obligatory subliminal reinforcement. Fortunately times were strange enough and stressful enough for him to accept just about anything he was told.

Verrana flawlessly maintained the stern façade of ruthless leader through the hangers, the base, and all while they were in the presence of the *Spacer* escort detail. As soon as the guard was dismissed though, and she was alone with Gaudynya, her demeanour changed in an instant. Gaudynya knew it would. She'd already sensed her barely contained anticipation. She walked straight up to her, and they kissed passionately.

'It's finally time for us to be together, Verrana. Tomorrow is the first day of the rest of our lives.'

Gaudynya pressed commitment and sincerity with everything she had and Verrana lit up from the inside, while she observed it from outside.

Is this what love looks like?

Verrana whispered, 'We're ready. I'm ready.'

Gaudynya kissed her again before stepping back and taking a seat. 'We don't have much time, Verrana. We need to go over the details and prepare ourselves.'

'You're right. We need to be focused. No more distractions please,' she said coyly.

Gaudynya gave her a *who me s*mile – always the method actor.

'We have a PT Hover with a capacity to put thirty bodies on the ground per drop. We'll have your whole unit within striking distance of Neam in less than two hours. We're going to drop the main force on the inner rec plains, right by the *Mainway*. As soon as the *EYE* realises it's happening, and responds, our reluctant allies in orbit will be forced to take out the strikers. There will be an overlap of course, and there will be casualties, but once that phase is over, we will be virtually unchallenged.'

'What about the Strikers from the southern stations?'

'The *Spacers* will take care of all her continental capacity in one go. It's going to be a sticky start Verrana, but after that, we're in. Everything revolves around Neam. It always has. It's the source of her Q-stream. When we have Neam, we have everything.'

Gaudynya could hardly keep herself from getting carried away. It was all so simple that once in motion, it couldn't fail. It would be a chain reaction no one could put a stop to.

'Are we going to fight alongside your own forces from the *Eastern Base*? Or operate independently?' Verrana queried.

'Our useable force here is only a hundred strong. I know it seems unfair, but we need to preserve that for the second phase. They simply won't be available in time before that anyway. We're depending on the courage and training of *SecCore*. Your force will be remembered in history as the liberators of humanity, Verrana.'

Verrana nodded, 'I understand. No victory without sacrifice. To be honest, it's probably for the best. We have a tactical route to the core and central. The *Sec* in the city will either join us or stand down – N-Canes are no match for what we can throw at them.'

'Precisely,' Gaudynya agreed. 'I've decided to bring in the *Outsiders* for the final phase. I know I can count on their support now. They will be invaluable for recovery in the aftermath.'

Verrana was surprised, but not too concerned. Her faith in Gaudynya was strong enough to trust her judgement. 'I'm sure you know what you're doing. I take it this has something to do with the little gift we delivered you, the Marcin woman?'

'She has every reason to try and make the best of the situation. One way or another though, she will be disappearing forever after. I'm going to make it crystal clear she has no part in the governance of this region or any other. She can serve her purpose, and then she can crawl back under her rock …and if I ever see her again, I will deal with her permanently.'

Verrana was surprised at Gaudynya's bitterness as she lost herself in the moment.

'Seems you've let her get under your skin. I don't know why, she's the past, irrelevant. We're the future, Gaudy. Some might have a soft spot for her, but she's never held any real power.'

She winced at Verrana's ridiculous shortening of her name, especially in combination with a reference to Marcin's inexplicable and equally ridiculous popularity.

'Verrana, just accept that she irks me and leave it at that.' She smiled, forced. 'When this is over, we will have outshone anything she ever achieved ...and then I'll be happy if you never mention her name again. With any luck it will disappear from history completely.'

. . .

Gaudynya had considered getting someone throw Marcin out of the gates. It wouldn't do though. She did deserve *some* respect, and she was sending her away still with a part to play. The least she could do was explain that part, and who else knew it? She strode into Quarantine with little attempt at hiding her impatience.

'Time for you to go, Marcin. The world changes forever tomorrow. Neam is about to fall, and the *EYE's* hold on this planet is about to be broken in a single day.'

Evelyn could feel she meant it. She certainly believed it.

'Fine with me. I never gave a moonrock about the *EYE*,' she answered casually.

Gaudynya was confused with her own contradicting emotions. Marcin had her uses here. On some level other than sex, she had an ounce of admiration for her. But by God, she did hate her!

'Just get lost, Marcin. I'm letting you go. Go to your idiot oaf and your nomadic wasters – and make sure they're ready for what's coming. Forty-eight hours from now the people in that city are going to need their help. I may even need their help.'

Evelyn raised an irreverent eyebrow. 'I knew I'd grow on you eventually, Gaudynya. Consider it done. My friend comes too. He busted me out of the city, least I can do is return the favour. I'm sure I can find a use for him.'

Gaudynya shrugged, 'The *1st*? Why not? Collect him on your way out. He can share your rations. I've spent enough time on you already.'

'Rations? You're making us walk?'

'You'll have plenty of time. You don't want to be anywhere near the city in the next few days. By the time you arrive, they will actually need you.'

I can't kill her if I'm not near her.

'Why don't you keep us here and just send word to *Infinity*. I could coordinate more effectively from here.'

Gaudynya laughed. No way she was sharing any glory of the front line. Especially not with Evelyn Marcin. 'I don't think so. And you don't want to. When it starts, our bridges are burned. It's the city or nothing for us both. This *Eastern Base* will be wiped off the face of the Earth too.'

'Wow. You mean you're going to have to lead from the front like a genuine old-world commander. How noble. I guess like you said though, there isn't much choice now.'

She glared… and Evelyn felt the full force of her sudden and ferocious rage! The hate roared, wrenching fear from the darkest corners of her mind. Her arms flailed to find something to hold on to. Flashing alien horrors overlayed her conscious self – sounds, not from her own memory, but from Gaudynya's. Pure brutality! Her mind and soul were being stabbed, over and over, shredding flesh and splintering bone. She reeled from a grotesque corpse, skin crumpling and blackening under the flame before her eyes, then from the face of a lifeless child staring unseeing at its lifeless mother, before morphing to a different face from her own past. *Terror… loneliness… hopelessness…* the flashes intertwined, driven entirely by Gaudynya. They closed and smothered, squeezing the life out of her …and there was no way out! Her chest felt crushed as she laboured for breath. She could taste blood, smoke …death.

Then the pressure and black smoke began to lift, and the room was suddenly too bright for her light-headedness. She was drained and breathless. Mostly though, relieved to have survived.

'I can crush you, Marcin. I wouldn't need to lift a finger, so go and serve your purpose …and know that if I ever see you again, I will.'

Evelyn reached for her own core, that thing Jeremy had tried to tell her about. Perhaps that was what she drew on now, a tether to something indestructible. All she had to do was hold onto it a little while longer, and not react. She watched Gaudynya's back as she strode away without another word. The door closed. She fell back into a seat, thoroughly drained and in shock.

Chapter Seventeen

Etta wasn't one for idling around the caves and HabFabs passing time on mundane aspects of everyday life. There was always a legitimate excuse to be on the back of a horse, whether that was a patrol, or just checking in with a neighbouring settlement. Today was going to no different. The patrols were already out, but she could still take a shift watching the *Eastern Base*. Drifting wouldn't suit Stan either, so she might as well see if he wanted to tag along. They were supposed to travel by two's anyway. They could be up at the hill in four hours.

. . .

'Why is it alright to be bored here but not back at the Caves, Etta?' Stan asked idly.

'For a start, I'm not bored. I'm doing something. Believe it or not, it might be something important. Strange times, Stan. Things are happening here.'

She still had the Field Enhance unit strapped around her head and over her eyes. For Stan it was uncomfortable after five minutes, Etta could happily wear it all day.

'So I hear,' he said with a hint of sarcasm.

'What, you disagree? You two turn up, and we never really got to the bottom of that. Your girlfriend's MIA, probably down there. There's a new *SecCore* division permanently camped outside of the city, apparently now in cohorts with a rogue *Spacer* Commander. There's an *Eastern Base* that appears to be completely quarantined even by its own people, probably due to said mind-altering, ego maniac *Spacer* Commander. *EYE* intel drones are running sorties all over the place. At what point do you start being concerned and concede that times are strange?'

'Strange isn't a word I use anymore. I'm not so much concerned about *the times* as I am with getting Evelyn back. If I find out for sure she's in there, I'll be a little more direct, don't worry about that.'

Etta was looking at him with the FE unit still over her eyes. At first, he thought she was going to launch into a rant about how he needed to focus and do as he was told, and not go half-cocked at the first sight of Evelyn. She took a deep breath though, and her response was all the more compassionate for it.

'I know,' she said. 'We'll get her back. Try and remember we're on the same side, Stan. You're going to need us when the time comes …and we're going to need you.'

. . .

He'd been dozing. The urgency in Etta's voice kicked the adrenaline in and brought him round with a start.

'Stan… Stan!! Wake up. They're out.'

'Wha…?'

'East gate. They just let them out …alone. It's Evelyn and Jeremy.'

He looked over, eyes straining as his hands fumbled with his own FE unit. 'Shass, let's just get down there.'

Etta put a hand on his shoulder. 'Not yet. They didn't break out. They're not being chased. Give it five minutes and see what happens, see which direction they head. Five minutes now will save us time.'

Her face was only inches from his, but her eyes were still covered with the unit. She took her hand away and leaned on the ridge again. He lay alongside her with his own unit now strapped over his eyes.

'It looks like they're heading this way, right toward our ridge,' he observed.

'Shass,' Etta whispered. 'They've probably always known we're here. They probably watch us as we watch them. I wouldn't be surprised if they pointed them in the right direction.'

'Might as well meet them,' Stan tried again.

'Or we might as well not,' Etta retorted. 'Don't you think she can make her own way up a hill? They'll be here in forty minutes if they know the way. We hold cover.'

. . .

Even when they were only a dozen yards away, Etta made Stan wait behind the ridge.

'It serves no purpose to give away your position unnecessarily,' she'd argued.

Evelyn's face eventually appeared over the rocks.

'I wanted to go down and meet you,' Stan told her straight away, sounding a little defensive.

Evelyn looked at him for a second, and then Etta.

'Why would you do that? I'm perfectly capable of walking up a hill by myself ...and this is such a cosy little spot.'

She was teasing them, and it seemed to be working a little too well. 'Seriously though, why would you? It would have been a waste of time. Speaking of which, that's something we don't have a lot of.'

'Why? What's going on?' Etta asked.

'Oh, the world's coming to an end tomorrow, unless we can do something about it. It's happening, kiddo's, Gaudynya and her new *SecCore* buddies are making a move on Neame.'

'Tomorrow? Are you sure? Neam isn't going fall to a washed-up excommunicated *Spacer* and a flaky *SecCore* division.'

Evelyn sat herself on a flat rock just as Jeremy finally appeared over the ridge and began explaining the situation.

'Gaudynya is a million miles from the Commander burnout you think she is – and if she is excommunicated, it's because that's exactly what she wants to be. This isn't the Middle Ages, Etta. There are no castle walls to knock down here. All she has to do is punch a hole in Central and she will have full control of the city ...and possibly the *EYE*.'

Jeremy slumped on a rock next to her in time to pick up the story. 'There's a good reason why the *EYE* didn't want Gaudynya in the city – and it's basically the same reason everyone else keeps their distance. The *EYE* has a surface routine. It's her personality, her appearance of sentience. Everything passes through it, in an abstract sense, and a large part of it connects to the implant tech of the 1st's. I think the idea was to learn how to be more human to work towards more direct control. If an individual 1st becomes too adept though, they can begin to influence the routine: *The Apex*. All the new 1st's have a failsafe now – there are more of them, but they are individually less powerful.   Gaudynya precedes that modification, and somehow, she managed to slip the net and get herself out the city. Not only that did she pull that trick off, but she also managed to position herself within the *Spacer* ranks. Her rise has been meteoric. By the time everyone realized just how powerful she was, how and why, it was almost too late. The fear is that now she knows what is possible, she might just be strong enough to take over the *personality* of the *EYE*. In effect, she would *become* the *EYE*.'

Etta wasn't convinced about Gaudynya's chances of getting back into the city. 'What about the Striker drones? The Stingers even?'

Evelyn filled them in on that scenario. 'We think the *Spacers* have the capacity to knock those out from orbit, and they would rather do that than risk losing their foothold on the surface. They don't want anyone to win or lose entirely. This weird unspoken three-way tolerance of one another in a delicate balance suits them …for now. It will be their hope to inflict limited damage on all sides and check any escalation. Afterwards they'll try to claim the neutral peacekeeping high ground. Gaudynya is supplying EMP cannons and pulse rifles to the *SecCore* pot too. She brought them with her from the *Island*. They'll go some way to neutralising the Stinger issue in the City.'

Etta was determined to go through the Devil's advocate motions. 'If all of that is true, what can we do?

To be honest, *why* would we want to do anything? There must be a high probability that Gaudynya will fail, and we're the last thing the *EYE* needs to worry about. Everyone has something to lose here but us. We might actually be left alone for a change.'

Evelyn was perfectly happy to be cross-examined. She could sense Etta was quite open on the subject. Her reservations were genuine.

'Everyone has something to lose, Etta. If Gaudynya really can break into this *Apex* thing, she'll be unleashing God-powerful Artificial Intelligence on the whole damned universe. The first thing she'll do is offer it up to the *Spacers,* in return for unlimited access to surface resources, and no doubt a seat at the head of their council too. She'll replace their founding principles with her own brand of conquest-model. She'll open the gates of the cities to let the people flood out without any clue or organisation. She wants as much chaos as possible, because that chaos will eventually bring her the power she craves. What she might do with it, and where it leads, who knows. All I do know is, there'll be no responsible control. All future off-world expansion will be sponsored by gatekeeping AI emperors answering to her, designed to do whatever *she* wants.'

It was a grim scenario to consider, and they all did. Evelyn sat at the centre of the contemplative huddle, taking a physical break after her hike up the hill, whilst also emotionally gauging the mood and resolve of her group. The undercurrent was a sense of indecision, especially from Etta. Jeremy and Stan would follow her anywhere, always ready to support, but Etta's outlook was more comparable to her own. She wasn't a soldier – she was a leader – which meant she had the weight of responsibility to contend with. On one level, she was reluctant to rely on *Evelyn Marcin* for anything, (partly due to how she felt about Stan now), but on another, there was hope – optimism for something brighter in the futures of *Infinity*. A little jealous rivalry wouldn't get in the way of the right decision.

They were as ready as they would ever be to accept how it was going to have to be.

'Ok, let me tell you the plan. Then you can tell me all the reasons you think it's a bad idea, and then I can explain again that it's the only idea.'

Stan grinned, 'Deja vous.'

'I know, right,' Evelyn smiled back, before being hit by another pang of resentment from Etta.

She ignored it and carried on. 'Timing is everything. I need to get to the core just ahead of Gaudynya. I can't walk in unchallenged, I can't go in the same way, and I certainly can't do it alone... which is why Jeremy is going to help me.'

She let that one sink in.

'If you think we're watching from the bench you have another thing coming, kiddo,' Stan told her flatly.

'We're a stretched for manpower. Etta needs to return and prepare *Infinity* for what's coming. There're a lot of people who will need their help after. And I need you down there when it starts,' she nodded toward the ridge they'd just walked over from the *Eastern Base*. 'Jeremy's more use in the city. There isn't a 1st anywhere that wouldn't recognise him in an instant – and that's the help I need. When it kicks off, they might even get the green light from you know who.'

'The base? Why do we need to send anyone back down there?' Etta asked.

'Once Gaudynya leaves on the warpath, they're on borrowed time at the *Eastern Base*. It will be flattened by the *Spacers* from orbit, along with the *EYE's* drone fields. You need to get them out before that happens. Get them to evacuate. Get them to join *Infinity* if you can. You need to be ready for that too. They should cooperate. Once this kicks off, things that were unthinkable before are suddenly going to seem like the best option.'

Stan was uncomfortable with pretty much all of it.

'Your part of this plan is pretty sketchy E. What about back-up for you?'

She knew he understood but she knew he needed to hear it anyway.

'This is the plan, Stan – and the back-up plan – and the backup backup plan. If I can't stop Gaudynya in the city, you guys need to be as ready and organised as you can for the shass storm that comes next.'

'What do you think about this?' he asked Jeremy. 'What are the odds of the city's *1st*'s deciding to sign up with a rebel icon and a rogue blue in a *SecCore* suit? Because it sounds like that's what it all hinges on.'

It was easy to forget sometimes that Jeremy, as well as being an Aqua *1st*, was also a man, and one who presumably valued his life as much as any other. He was clearly physically fatigued by recent events but seemed mentally at ease with the circumstances. He'd been a feature in Evelyn's life during her previous return to twenty-nine, so Stan was predisposed to see him as trustworthy. He was getting a sense for himself now that he was a fair, objective, and humbly courageous human being.

Jeremy answered in his measured way, 'It's the best and only option. That isn't an endorsement of probable success though. It's a priority for people already outside to get a heads-up. Tomorrow's going to be a tough day for everyone. There's no precedent to predict how we're going to fare inside …I'm going on faith.'

He was looking at Evelyn and smiling a kind of gallows smile. Stan swelled with pride. Etta tried not to roll her eyes. Evelyn just felt the too familiar flush of hero embarrassment.

'God help us,' she mumbled.

'I second that,' Etta added.

Stan laughed heartily, 'I'm in then. We don't need God – we have Evelyn Marcin!'

She gave him a look to say – *I can't believe you went there. I hate you right now. You're a complete di…*

But it's difficult to hate someone when you can feel the pure love, hope and joy behind their words. She even sensed the acceptance and respect from Etta. She was attracted to Stan, as he was to her – but it wasn't love. It wasn't anything like what they had. Etta had a higher cause anyway, and an admirable one at that – commitment to her people. The *pattern* reminded her a lot of Helaine's.

'Let's do this,' she said. 'Don't worry about precedents and guesses, just get in there and get on with it, Marcin. We'll be ready for anything when you're finished.'

She looked at Stan too. 'You both take care. You need to get through this,' with a nod in the direction of Evelyn's abdomen to clarify her meaning. 'I'm going. Hopefully we'll all meet again soon … and good luck!'

She accepted the farewells of the other three and set off on her way without ceremony. They watched her go until she descended a dip and disappeared out of sight.

'We'll be going that way too, Jeremy. Why don't you get a head start? I'll catch up.'

Evelyn needed a moment with Stan. She needed much more than that, but a precious minute was all they had for now.

He got up stiffly and moved to shake Stan's hand. It looked like he was trying to think of something meaningful to say but all he managed was, 'See you soon, my friend. Good luck.'

He disappeared into the same dip Etta had moments before, and suddenly everything was different. They were together again, and alone again. It was a feeling Evelyn loved and knew Stan did too. At times like this they were insulated from the nonsense of the universe. They were safe. They were whole. It was almost in defiance of nature to be so content. They kissed and held each other quietly ...but it wasn't just the two of them this time. She knew he could feel that too.

'You should go,' he whispered eventually. He sounded upbeat and confident though. More so than he felt. 'If you don't catch J soon, he'll be eaten by some small mammal or pecked to death by a bird.'

'Don't worry, he's more resilient than you give him credit for, and your nowhere near as confident as you'd like me to believe.'

'Yeah, I guess there's no fooling you now.'

He seemed thoughtful and concerned, aware that she might pick up insecurity on a different level.

'Some things are different, Stan, but all the important things are still the same. It's going to take some getting used to is all ...and that insecurity has always been an occupational hazard for us *Shifty* folk. Don't think that because you can't see mine that it isn't there. It is. We'll work it out though.'

'Thing is, the second I don't feel like working it out, you'll already know. How will I know if you change your mind?'

She gave him the look. 'You'll know, kiddo.'

Then it softened. 'I'm not the string along or tag along type, but I can't imagine anything changing what we are.'

He held her again, tighter this time. After a minute she could feel his mental pattern shifting into game face mode. He'd resolved to let her go, to do what she had to do. He had his own mission too.

He stepped back. 'Ok, we're good. Let's get on with this, kiddo.'

She punched his shoulder. 'Yeah, let's do this, kiddo.'

Chapter Eighteen

'Are you in communication range yet, J? I don't even know if I'm enabled in that way. How would I use it if I were?'

They'd reached the eastern perimeter of the outer rec zone and had already found an access route. All they needed now was some form of transport, and that was going to mean announcing themselves.

'I wouldn't know about you,' he answered. 'And I wouldn't worry about it either. Signal's fine here, and the *EYE* already knows we're here.'

'Well? Is she going to lay on some transport or drop a charge on us? Feet have got us about as far as they can. If we can't get transport, it will take another two days to get to the core.'

'Hold on,' he said.

There was the pause again and that familiar blank expression on his face. They were definitely in comms range with the *EYE*.

'We're five miles from an unmanned station with a covered overlander, or twenty-five miles from a manned outpost that could pick us up.'

She calculated for a second. 'Quicker for them to come to us. I'm fine with that. We can rest while we wait. We need help from other 1st's along the line too. Get them to work out an intercept and meet us on the way. As many as she can spare. They're going to be more useful with me than they will be anywhere else anyway.'

Jeremy went blank again for a moment, then he raised an eyebrow as if he were mildly surprised. 'Consider it done. They're on their way with the transport, and our other 1st's will rendezvous en route to the core.'

'I say what I mean, and I mean what I say, Jeremy. The *EYE* knows this. She also knows I have a very good reason not to screw her over …unfortunately. I don't think Gaudynya dropping by is going to be an enormous surprise either. *EYE* knows the shass is about to hit the fan. She'll see us as a useful weapon in reserve.'

'Speaking of …shass, and fans, how long do you think we have?' he asked matter-of-factly. He was almost getting as used to this as she was.

She made light of her reply too. 'Well, I would say all the fans are in position and running at full speed, so I expect the shass will be arriving anytime. Hopefully it will hold off long enough for us to be in a covered vehicle with a squad of able 1st's.'

. . .

Jonas prepared for the announcement. His temples were thudding from the adrenaline. He found he was trying to move what little moisture he had left around his mouth. His hair was virtually standing on its own. He sat down in front of the monolithic photo-converter and adjusted himself.

'Prime Representative, this is it. It's begun,' he announced to the image that appeared slightly brighter than his own rooms setting.

'Well then, we've been over this enough. If the engagement threshold is confirmed, there is no further reason to delay,' she answered stoically.

'The *SecCore* force is on the move by ground and air, focusing their assault from the west along the *Mainway*. Bold and direct. Very Gaudynya. We're locked onto the *EYE's* Strikers. Just waiting for the first sign of movement from there.'

There was a slight hesitation before he concluded his update.

'There is one other thing …but I see no reason why it should alter our planned action now.'

The prime representative pinched the bridge between her eyes, the stress of the situation clearly affecting her. 'Go on.'

Jonas was mindful of making sure nothing in his tone would influence the significance of the statement.

'Evelyn Marcin has re-entered the boundary of Neam on the eastern side. She is accompanied by one other person, the man who she escaped the city with. I only mention it because some viewed her as a person of interest in the past, not because I believe she has any significance here today.'

The Prime Representative stared unfocused at an area out of view as she considered it. She shook her head with a hint of resignation when she eventually responded.

'I must agree …for now. She stays in the intel schedule though, and I want her progress included in updates routinely.'

'Of course. If there's nothing else, I should return to command now.'

The prime Representative stared at him compassionately before signing off.

'This is on all of our shoulders, Jonas. Your hand is our hand. What you do, you do with the full support of the council.'

. . .

Etta arrived back at the *Infinity Corp's* sleepy centre of administration, such as it was in hillside caves surrounded by an assortment of HabFabs covered in mud and sticks for camouflage. She had known before her recent detention what a city looked like. She had been raised and completed her Base of Knowledge in Neam. Their mother had only taken them out to the settlement project when she was seventeen. Emii had been nineteen. It had certainly taken some getting used to life outside. Hard to believe. There was no going back now, not as far as she was concerned.

Reassuringly she had been picked up by a perimeter patrol, but even thinking about that, she realised if anyone had ever made a serious attempt, they could easily have been wiped from the Earth long before now.

Helaine had just returned from a run and hadn't changed or cooled down yet. Her sweat-soaked vest showed how toned she was for her age.

'I wasn't expecting you back so soon, Etta …or alone. I take it you're here to give me something else to think about,' she said.

'Plenty, I'm afraid. Where's Emii?'

'I've sent for her already. Probably be an hour or two though. She's out in the southern subs.'

Helaine was giving her a strange look with a raised eyebrow. 'Apparently she has a *friend* out there.'

Etta had heard about that. She'd never met him though, and for some reason they never spoke about it. She realised it was a strange situation.

'Yes, I heard there was someone. That's about all I know.'

Helaine raised an eyebrow again. 'What kind of a sister doesn't ask about a thing like that?'

'One who is more concerned with all of us staying alive.'

Helaine would always make her point no matter what else was happening in the world. 'Staying alive means being alive. Life is more than just survival, Etta. Do you think caring for someone like that is a weakness?'

It was a million miles away from what she had come to discuss, and it was already annoying. Wouldn't it be nice if everyone could be with a perfect person, and when you were lucky enough to find that perfect person, they weren't already with another perfect person. She was annoyed with herself for allowing the thought into her head, especially now!

'Great Sky above, Helaine, I didn't run all the way back here for a lecture on boyfriends. The worlds about to be thrown into chaos. Ours, the *Spacers*, the city, all of it – starting from today. That's what I brought back for you to think about.'

Helaine wasn't one for running around in blind panic with her face in her hands. Her moment of serene thoughtfulness in response to the news came as no surprise to Etta. She always had been a rock.

'So, it has started already? Who is the aggressor?' she asked calmly.

'Gaudynya, obviously. She's turned the northern *SecCore* division under commander Verrana Rhone into her own personal strike force. If it hasn't started yet we're only hours or minutes away. Evelyn was being held at the *Eastern Base* as we suspected. Gaudynya just released her so that she could give us the heads up. She actually expects our cooperation in picking up the pieces after. Can you believe that?'

'And Evelyn? Where is she now?'

Etta resisted the urge to roll her eyes. She understood why she felt the way she did, and it wasn't helpful. 'Where you would think she'd be, in the thick of it. She made straight for the city with the *1st* she knows. Stan is going to warn the *Spacers* left behind in the *Eastern Base* of its imminent and very permanent decommissioning. If he's successful they may be arriving here too. One way or another we need to prepare ourselves as best we can for a massive influx of refugees. Eve's hope is that we'll work with the *Eastern Spacers* to try and coordinate that.'

Helaine nodded. 'Good. They will have skills and personnel we can use. If we are really lucky, they might even bring some useful equipment with them. We need to gather and brief everyone and get word out to the subs. We'll use this place as a reception hub to direct any incomers. We should assemble a small task force of our own too. I would like to get some back up to Evelyn if possible.'

Etta wasn't looking at her now. She was looking past and above her. Helaine turned to see what had caught her attention. Two smoke trails from the high atmosphere ended their journey by dispersing into two clouds of peppery specs that scattered like seeds on a breeze.

Etta whispered, 'Only minutes to impact. I hope he's out of there.'

. . .

Things had gone more smoothly than Stan could have hoped. He had their attention. There was no way he could have made it to the gate without being noticed even if he wanted to, and once they had him inside it was literally only a matter of minutes before the administrator, Thonsen, was all over it and trying to figure out the situation. They were already in a state of high alert after Gaudynya's swift and unannounced exit with both their PT hovers and a team of base personnel. What Stan had to tell him wasn't actually going to sound so unbelievable in light of that. Thonsen had gotten used to the idea in recent weeks that they were pretty much on their own regarding communications and assistance from off-world anyway.

'I have to be really direct, man. You don't have time to work out who's who or any kind of plan. This place is ash. Everything and everyone needs to be out in one hour. I'd prefer it to be a lot less. Evacuate everyone who can't carry anything right now. A few of us can maybe spend the next thirty minutes grabbing some gear.'

Thonsen hadn't reacted with astounded and indignant disbelief. Things had been unstable for weeks, if not months. He knew Stan was a man with a plenty to lose. He was also a man who would try and do the right thing. It made sense. An Administrator turning his base inside out certainly wasn't in any play book – not in this timescale, and not on the unsubstantiated word of an *Outsider*. He knew in his bones that Stan was right though, and he wasn't going to risk letting everyone burn when their own people had already cut them off.

'We have nothing else to lose,' he had told Stan. 'The worse that can happen is we lose faster. It looks as if we are all going to end up on *Team Marcin* after all.'

. . .

The scene in front of Evelyn and Jeremy was almost comedic. A group of *1st*s milled around five Personal Ground Vehicles, all dressed in their totally impractical and inappropriate aqua gowns. Usually they were only seen alone or in pairs, as unperturbable beacons of stability and control. Even as they approached, it was obvious that this group were now anything but.

'I'd say by the look on their faces that the shass is well and truly underway already,' Evelyn said.

Jeremy didn't answer. He was focused on the group, working out who was there and how things were going to play. As their overlander pulled up just short of them, he opened his door. He was already walking toward them as he turned to speak to Evelyn. 'Wait here one moment.'

It clearly wasn't a discussion. He strode off before she could answer. She watched as he chose one to approach and the others gathered around.

Who could have imagined a sight like this? A dozen nervous *1st's* in a team huddle with an old guy in a stolen *SecCore* uniform.

After five minutes of conferring that seemed to be led by an uncharacteristically assertive Jeremy, he walked back to the overlander.

'They're ready to meet you now. I've explained a little about the situation regarding your implants. Just go slowly with them. The best way is to be open about anything you do. Somehow you have to get them to trust you, and you're not going to be able to just *persuade* a dozen *1st's*.'

'I get it, Jeremy. Thanks for smoothing the way. I was thinking something along the same lines anyway.'

He looked at them and nodded as if to say, *ok, here she comes.*

'Alright,' he said. 'Let's get to know each other. I'm not worried at all.'

He seemed genuinely more concerned than she was. She was tempted to calm him but considering what they'd just discussed it seemed a little inappropriate. He would be fine. He was intelligent, had a high level of self-control …and yes, her old favourite – the same completely unfounded faith everyone else had in her! She got out and followed him.

As they approached, everything would have appeared normal from a conventional perspective. For Evelyn though, things were happening on a different sensory level. She could feel the potential on the other side of their collective *wall*, and as they drew closer it began to burst through in undisciplined flashes. They were like a pack of half-trained dogs. They knew what they were supposed to do, but they also knew what they would rather do! It was like having to hold her hands in the air while they leaped and snapped at her.

Jeremy studied her. 'Ok?' he asked.

She answered calmly, making sure her emotions were as level, neutral, and as open as possible. 'No. Do you think we could all just calm the rock down? What happened to taking things slow? I thought we agreed it wasn't going to be a mass mind molestation. Everyone brick it in for a minute please and keep it conventional …until we've been introduced at least!'

Jeremy gave them an admonishing look of disappointment. 'Did any of you receive an order to specifically hinder this woman's progress? No? Were you requested to meet here and assist in any way you can? I think you were. Let's be clear and confirm the chain of command here. We are on the same side. You answer to me. I answer to her. Now you will allow her to make sure you understand.'

Evelyn, out of courtesy, allowed them the opportunity to consent vocally first. After a few seconds had passed one of them spoke for the group. The mental pushing and shoving had already ceased.

'We apologize. The events and circumstances of our meeting clouded our judgement. We will calm our minds now and allow you to explore our intent,' he said nobly.

It occurred to her that trust was a two-way street, and that she was the odd one out here. There seemed no harm in pointing that out.

'Look, you're either with me or you're not. I have nothing to lose at this point and no way to change your minds if you're against me. I don't have the time, and I can't spare the energy. Read me …but be respectful about it. I stand for the citizens of Neam. I stand for people wherever they are. I stand for you too …and I need your help!'

She took the equivalent of a mental deep breath – focusing on her intentions while keeping her mind as open as possible. The different patterns began to drift in, more patient and courteous this time. She found she was able to associate them with the corresponding physical person. It was working better than she had anticipated, serving as an orderly mental introduction. Without exception, each of the patterns left more positive than it had arrived, and more than that, they were feeding back into a growing stream of shared confidence.

Jeremy watched her again. 'Are we good?' he asked cautiously.

'We are. We all are. In fact, I think we might be better than good.'

Chapter Nineteen

The *EYE's* response was following the script to the letter. Gaudynya was feeling like a grand master with the upper hand, closing in on an inevitable checkmate. Her forces had exploded into the built-up areas of the city and scattered like shrapnel. They had divided into dozens of small and deadly focus units with individual objectives that would contribute to the ultimate victory. Many of the missions were simply distractions, inflicting maximum damage to soft and sensitive targets to confuse and overwhelm the automatic responses. The packs of tiny stinger drones that had swarmed around the first squads were now spread thinly over a massive area, and they were effectively redundant under the covered sections. Striker drones, the *EYE's* big guns, had been launched with predictable AI efficiency – a measured response plus a small percentage contingency, leaving most of the force safely grounded in reserve. They hit the *apparent* spearhead of Gaudynya's forces with devasting accuracy, as she knew they would …but by the time they had finished there was nowhere for them to return to, and nothing left of the reserves that had been held back on the ground. From her position in the north-eastern wild rec zone, Gaudynya had watched the re-entry plumes of the *Spacers'* carrier pods seconds before dispersing their lethal cargo. She had watched the tell-tale black smoke rise behind the hills, and she had waited for the sound of the distant thunder that she knew would follow. It hadn't been confirmed yet, but she strongly suspected the same fate had befallen her own *Eastern Base*. The bridges were well and truly burned now …the only direction left was forward.

Her two partners in the city's downfall stood at her side – her right hand, *SecCore* Commander Verrana Rhone – and her left, faithful disciple Saska. She was only a pilot, but how well she had played her part! Verrana undoubtably loved her in her way, but Saska was something else. The depth of loyalty and regard she had was far beyond her own comprehension.

'I think it's time for you to clear my path to Central, Verrana. Today is the first day of a new future for us all.'

Verrana was staring arrogantly at Saska while replying to Gaudynya. 'It will be an honour, my love …and don't worry, I'll take good care of little Saska.'

They despised each other. It was clear enough on the surface, but on a subliminal level it was much more intense. Verrana was a tease and a bully and viewed Saska as competition for Gaudynya's affection. Saska's hatred of Verrana was different, less selfish. She merely thought of Verrana as unworthy. They certainly weren't ever going to be able to live and work together, which meant eventually she would have to make a choice. The decision would be easy enough of course. What Verrana offered, apart from her current military status, could be found anywhere – desire was the easiest emotion to amplify. What Saska had was either there or it wasn't though, something rare and inexplicable …perhaps it *was* love. Whatever it was, she knew it was something she would miss more. Saska hadn't reacted because she hadn't needed to. She only had one mistress.

Ignoring Verrana now, Gaudynya spoke only to Saska. 'Today's victory will be in no small part thanks to you, Sas. You have been my rock. Help Verrana take Central. You deserve to be there too. You should be with us at the end.'

Verrana wasn't the only one who could tease and bully. Her jealousy and hate flared lava-red just beneath the surface. It was an effort for Gaudynya to find something else in there to restore her equilibrium. Eventually she did manage to cool the fire and was annoyed with herself for having started it in the first place. She needed to conserve energy, not waste it on lovers' quarrels.

. . .

Evelyn had a sense of what was coming; a gut feeling too vague and too late to be useful.

'Shass,' she whispered.

Their lead vehicle buckled and exploded without flame, pretty much disintegrating to nothing recognisable.

'H.E.D. mine!' screamed one of the *1st's*.

Conventional small calibre fire followed, slamming into the front and rear vehicles.

She was almost relieved. It was a small unit, probably four forgotten city *SecCore* detailed to watch a backway. If they'd known who the convoy was carrying it might well have been a larger force, and they might have all ended simultaneously like the first.

Everyone's instincts were the same – pull out and go back the way they had come – it would have been fatal though.

'Everyone floor it, forward only. They're behind us already,' Evelyn shouted into the open comm.

Their new lead vehicle sped ahead taking fire from the one gun that had been left directly in front. The other three *SecCore* had taken positions further back anticipating a retreat. The new point vehicle, the one just ahead of Evelyn's, suddenly swerved and slammed sideways into the building corner where the fire was coming from, blocking the opening and causing the lone *Sec* to fall back.

'Keep moving. We'll hold here,' advised a new voice over the comm. It was Gabriel, another of the *1st's*. These people were not soldiers. His prospects weren't good if stayed where he was.

'Thanks Gabriel,' she answered as they passed. 'You've done enough. Get out if you can. You know where we're going if you can get there.'

'I do, and I will,' he answered simply.

'Still some work to do here by the look of things.' It was Stella, another of the *1st's*, but from the back of the convoy. 'We'll attempt to rendezvous again at the core.'

Evelyn was grateful for her initiative. It was an order she would have been reluctant to give, for an action that was probably necessary.

'Thanks Stella. Make sure you do, alright.'

She looked at Jeremy with an expression that said everything she felt – thank you, I'm sorry, I had to, and we're not all going to make it …and maybe none of us will.

His response was a strained smile. 'You made an impression. They're *all in*, as you would say. Let's not waste it. It will be your turn soon enough.'

It will. Am I kidding myself though? Am I really up to this?

As if he had heard her thoughts he added, 'We can do this. You can do this.'

She just smiled back.

I hope you're right.

· · ·

The blockade wasn't meant to be subtle. Word had gone ahead, and they weren't taking any chances. An armoured riot barrier had been secured across the sub-route. Four *SecCore* vehicles were parked behind it. Considering events on the other side of the city it was probably all they could spare here. Unfortunately though, it was also more than enough to hold back two light civilian vehicles and their six lightly armed and inexperienced occupants.

'What do you think?' Jeremy asked.

'I think we're not going any further this way. Trouble is, if we move, they'll move too. We'll be like a pawn trying to pass through a wall of pawns,' she answered.

'Do you have anything resembling a plan?'

She didn't quite roll her eyes, but she did let out an exaggerated sigh. 'Obviously. It isn't perfect though. I was hoping to have the mental firepower of these guys to fall back on at the core, not waste it here.'

'So you're going on alone?'

'No choice. But on the positive side, by the looks of this lame blockade there shouldn't be too much opposition on the other side.'

'Apart from Gaudynya,' he reminded unnecessarily.

'Walk in the park, I'm sure.'

She turned to Anton who seemed to have become the unofficially appointed leader of the remaining *1st's*.

'You know what you need to do, right? You don't have to break through, just get their attention and keep it. Don't be overly passive either. They have to believe you're trying.'

'Yes. We've all had similar basic tactical training to *SecCore* at some point. For most of us it wasn't a recent experience, but it will serve nonetheless,' he said.

'Good. You know, if you can get a couple of bodies up in these Res blocks, you'll almost be flanking them. You should be able to keep them pinned here, even with small arms fire. They might have considered that too though, so tell your guys to be careful if you try it. Ok, let's get this started so I can be on my way.'

Within minutes they launched an offensive in a fashion that shook even Evelyn. Two of the *1st's* set one of their PGV's in motion, and then clung to the back of it! They scrambled to the roof just before it made contact with the barrier. As they hit, they were thrown clean over, landing right among the stunned *SecCore*. In the ensuing firestorm two other *1st's* blasted their way into the Res blocks on either side. The two over the barricade probably only lasted around thirty seconds but had only intended to focus the *SecCore* attention. Before the *Sec* had had chance to re-evaluate, the *1st's* in the blocks were already in position and raining fire down. Evelyn retreated on foot to find a suitable side-route to take her around. It would be easy enough now. Most regular citizens would be following advice and staying inside. Anyone not heeding that advice would assume she was no different to them. As for *SecCore*, they were too thinly spread to be roaming the side-routes. They would only be acting on specific intelligence anyway, and presumably, they weren't getting that from their usual source right now – the *EYE*.

She tried to make her avoidance of other citizens subtle. Her top garment incorporated a hood. It wasn't unusual to wear one in the open sections and it helped to conceal her identity. How necessary that was here, she wasn't sure – all she knew was she didn't need further complications right now. She paused at an intersection to consider the best route – ahead and to the right looked like another footway maze that headed roughly in the right direction – fifty yards to the left though looked like a slipway onto a main core D-route.

The surprise of a voice so close behind her almost took her breath away. Nothing threatening in it, she just hadn't realised anyone was there …which was unusual.

'You scared the shass out me!'

The girl shrugged. She was twenty at most. The age when a young woman could still look unphased by the total chaos unfolding in her home city.

'Sorry. I thought I might know my way around better than you. You looked like you were considering the D. Take it from me, it's a busy day on the D.'

'Busy how?'

'Busy with people interested in anyone who thinks they have business at the core, like you.'

Evelyn's eyes narrowed as she considered the girl and whether she'd recognised her …*yes, clearly, she does*.

'Evelyn Marcin. Yes, I know who you are. Don't worry, I'm more than happy for you to carry on with whatever you're doing here.'

'So it seems,' Evelyn agreed. 'Normally people don't get that close without me knowing. I'm a little impressed. How did you manage it?'

'I must be light on my feet.'

'It's not your feet I'm concerned about, it's your mind. What's the deal, kiddo?'

Pleased with herself, a little smug even, very competently controlled anxiety – a reasonable slice of admiration for me. As minds go, kid pretty much has the sport model.

'You read too, don't you?' the girl asked her. 'You're good. I can't even feel it.'

'You're pretty competent yourself. I wouldn't expect that of someone so young. I certainly wasn't expecting to bump into it here.'

'I'm a novitiate. A potential 1st. It's a relatively knew thing.'

There was pride in her vocalisation, but it was supported in her emotional thread too.

'Listen…'

'Zenna. Zenna Mira.'

'…ok, Zenna Mira…'

Evelyn hesitated. Could she be useful? Do I have any right to expect her to be?

Zenna brought the matter to the conventional level. 'You need my help, and you're conflicted about asking for it. I don't have to read that – I can see it on your face. I'll do what I can for you. I don't know how much use I can be or how far I want to go though.'

Evelyn shrugged. 'Fair enough. Let's take a minute first. I'm going to make myself as open as I can so you can take a look and get to know me, warts and all. Take your time, ok ...and don't be shy.' She reinforced some confidence with the last part. Of course she was going to feel uncomfortable, blatantly rummaging around someone else's mind, especially a mind more experienced and more enhanced than her own.

Without speaking Zenna reached in cautiously. Evelyn relaxed as she had with the other 1st's. She cleared all conscious thought and settled into the deep and silent well of herself. Zenna's alien pattern appeared and dissolved in different areas without encouragement or resistance as it queried respectfully. Evelyn didn't follow it or judge its choices and processes. Eventually she just realised the pattern wasn't there anymore.

'Are you ok?' Evelyn asked her.

Zenna looked like she'd had a life changing epiphany – that or seen a ghost!

Evelyn shook her head. 'Beats the devil out of me what people think they see in there that's so ...whatever it is that makes a person's face do that.'

Zenna's eyes had actually overflowed, and a tear rolled shamelessly down her cheek.

'I know. You mustn't try and read it either, Evelyn Marcin. You have to trust me as I trust you.'

'I do. I'm guessing it's not entirely a coincidence that you're here too?' she enquired simply.

Zenna wiped her cheek. 'This way.'

Chapter Twenty

Zenna led them into the maze of residential sub-ways. They were getting closer to central though. These buildings housed *Alpha's*, highest of the four status grades. The overhead coverings were staged above on multiple levels and enclosed link-ways criss-crossed between blocks. Evelyn found this area of the city the most claustrophobic, and least welcoming! The *Alpha's* superior attitude wasn't only tolerated, it seemed it was positively encouraged, probably as a kind of calculated aspirational motivator – if a lower-class citizen towed the line long enough, one day they too might live the conceited *Alpha* dream.

Sticking to ground level they were mostly alone, or at least ignored when they weren't. There had been one larger group of around twenty or so locals milling around and looking confused. A couple of them had shouted over but hadn't pursued the strangers walking purposefully by on the other side.

At last, the matrix came to an end, and between the last pair of res blocks the landscape opened to a brightly lit circle of reflective ceramic ground. The glowing floor ran around the full circumference of the domed core, punctuated only with contrasting dark-grey pedestrian features. It was the Staging-way. Over on the other side, the river of light seemed to run straight down into the dome-covered chasm of the three sub-terranean levels. The reality that couldn't be seen from here though was the maze of ramps, walk-ways and elevators just below eye-level.

'Ok, only the small matter of crossing one of the most exposed spaces on the planet. Any thoughts of how we might go about that, Zenna?'

Zenna raised her eyebrows and shrugged, but at least she hadn't just turned around and walked away.

'Yeah, me either. I think we're about opposite the east-twelve bridgeway but it's likely to be well guarded. That's probably the least of our worries though. There's absolutely no way we can make it across there unchallenged. Question is, will they shoot on sight, or detain us?'

Zenna raised her brow again. 'You're thinking you can *persuade* your way in?'

'Not me ...*we*. I think I stumbled onto something last time I was outside the city, last time I got detained. Ironically, it was in an unenhanced mind, something natural. The fact that it was unmodified makes it even more interesting. It was a kind of synchronisation of will that allowed for an openness I could benefit from. It was fleeting, but it was definitely there, like a booster.'

Zenna had guessed something like this might be on the cards from when Evelyn had allowed her to read her. There had been no attempt to disguise the fact that if she went along, Evelyn was going to make use of her in ways other than just directions.

'I've barely begun with this. You know I'm only in my first year. Tell me what you want Evelyn, and I will try. I just don't want you to be disappointed.'

'Come off it, Zenna. I'm sure plenty of people have told you already, but I'll say it again if you need to hear it… You're special. You've got aptitude and attitude in spades. As minds go, you got the pro-sport model, and you know it – and if you know it, the *EYE* knows it, so you probably got the headgear to match.'

Zenna wasn't bashful about it. The shrug and subliminal messages that came with it were saying – *Yeah, I am kind of something. Glad you noticed!*

'Ok, what do you need?' She asked with renewed confidence. 'Should we go back and find someone to practice on first.'

'We don't have that luxury. You're going to have to learn on the job. This about trust, Zenna. You and I are one purpose now. My pattern is yours, and yours is mine. There must be no resistance, no disagreement, no questioning, no doubting. You need to maintain a *no mind* state. Follow me, and concentrate only on me …especially my will. My will is your will – accept it and feed it back. I'm hoping you have the subtlety to vary the intensity too. It must feel natural. And you need to stay hidden. I don't want to be distracted because I have to protect you.'

They turned their attention to the exposed expanse ahead, physically and metaphorically. The Staging-way was a quarter of a mile wide – a five-minute walk in a straight line. They were under no illusions about their chances of covering a single minute of that unchallenged though. If the challenge came as a kill-order, that was it, end of the road. If the emphasis was capture, they had a chance. It was a gamble – and the only option.

'Shall we?' Evelyn asked, cheerfully and politely.

'After you,' Zenna replied, smiling nervously.

. . .

'Look! Over there, it's Evelyn! What on Earth is she thinking?' Etta exclaimed.

'She's thinking that *SecCore* are thinking they're walking out to pick up two little girls, and they're about to get a big surprise,' Stan beamed with an excited smile. 'It's time to make some noise, Etta …shall we?'

'Follow me,' Etta replied cheerfully, as she unshouldered her weapon and began firing into the air.

Jeremy covered his ears and stepped back as the rest of the *Infinity Corps* took up positions in front of him. For a moment his instinct was to ask for a weapon of his own and contribute the fight. Without realising why though he stopped to check with the unofficial leader of their band of rebel *1st's*. He was waving him back from the action.

'We may be more productive elsewhere. It is possible we may be able to follow her into the core amidst the distraction. If nothing else, we will serve to add to the chaos from a different angle,' he shouted.

Jeremy realised he was right. *1st's* were a wasted resource in a gun fight when they might prove far more useful on the inside. Stan and Etta were too busy now to be bothered with their plans.

He nodded, 'Absolutely. Let's go.'

. . .

The six-strong *SecCore* unit that had been heading to intercept Evelyn and Zenna with their weapons raised suddenly turned and instinctively lowered into battle-ready stances. The two women they had been sent to deal with for wandering across the Staging-way were instantly forgotten.

Evelyn grabbed Zenna's hand and led her on a course to go around them with a wide margin.

'Do you have to look so calm, Zenna? We're supposed to be panicked citizens.'

She bowed her head and hunched as Evelyn pulled her along.

'What do you suppose is happening over there?' she asked.

'I'm sure I couldn't imagine,' Evelyn replied coyly.

'Your boyfriend I take it? Is he known for being this subtle?'

'He has his moments,' she smiled.

Two armoured *SecCore* vehicles rolled slowly off the east-twelve bridgeway shielding twelve of their personnel who were on foot. They were heading very directly toward the source of fire …towards Stan! It was the only angle they needed to worry about – other units would be converging from every direction, now that their position had been revealed. Stan and his group were the sole focus of *SecCore* now, and the two female citizens would just have to fend for themselves.

'Come on. We're the least of anyone's concerns, and time just became even more of an issue,' Evelyn said. She pulled Zenna's hand to raise the pace to an energetic jog. She soon had to slow again though as she realised that despite her lack of complaining, Zenna wasn't fit enough to keep it up.

They slowed to a brisk walk to recover their breathing as they arrived at the east-twelve bridgeway and resumed the panicked citizen act.

'Might be easier to find a quiet step-way to the lower levels and make our way up from inside,' Zenna suggested.

Evelyn took a moment to assess her state of mind. 'It's ok. We'll be fine. We don't have time for detours. Remember what we talked about. I need the Zen Zenna, ok. *Trust… faith… control*. Focus on me.'

She was reinforcing the words with their true essence. Not covertly though, in a way that invited Zenna to join and reciprocate.

She did. She amplified the feedback of positive trust and faith …and it worked! The fact that it worked was encouraging, and that too became part of the cycle.

'Remember, you *are* me. Follow me constantly and forget yourself. Whatever happens, don't panic. Keep your focus with me.'

Zenna nodded blankly.

Half-way over the bridge and they were putting theory into practice. The aqua forms of two confused *1st's* had appeared to challenge them, accompanied by a single armed *SecCore* operative. As the operative began to question them, they both felt the familiar and expected mental invasion of the *1st's*. They were careful not to resist and presented them only with the foggy soup of confusion that two frightened citizens would naturally feel. They managed to look the part easily enough! The *1st's* had already had enough confusion for one day and quickly lost interest.

One of them addressed the *Sec* dismissively. 'Just hold them somewhere …or let them inside even.'

It would have been easy enough to influence the *Sec* to take the latter option. They couldn't risk it in front of two *1ˢᵗ's* though. He had to make up his own mind, and he chose the option that was going to complicate matters and delay them further. They had no choice but to play along and wait for an opportunity.

. . .

The *Infinity Corps* had no reason to be masters of urban warfare – but it wasn't as alien as one might have thought. They were used to hiding, used to finding and making the most of cover, used to thinking on their feet with limited options ...and used to relying on a belief in their cause and faith in each other. The interconnected *Alpha* blocks at the edge of the staging-way were ideal for cover, giving the more numerous but exposed *SecCore* limited targets. The small force on the staging-way ahead was effectively pinned down. But it was the backways that were becoming increasingly difficult to manage – only a matter of time before they would be overrun. *Infinity's* eventual downfall seemed inevitable, but the outcome of their objective was not ...all they needed to win was time.

. . .

It was an effort to hide their frustration as the time ran down. They were just too close to the *SecCore* operative, who had now been joined by a second. The two aqua *1ˢᵗs* were also near enough to detect any mental interference. Evelyn was beginning to accept that a physical exchange seemed inevitable at this point. She was working on a course of action when the break they'd been hoping for appeared on the bridgeway. Her posse of rogue 1st's were casually walking across it in a regimented double line formation looking the embodiment of city authority. The two Aqua's assigned to watch the bridgeway now focused entirely on their approaching comrades, postures alert and attentive as they smoothed and checked their robes. Evelyn enforced similar intense concentration in the minds of the *SecCore* guards. The Intensity of events being what they were, that state of mind would hold until well after they had escaped into the vastness of the core.

Sneaking away, she felt a momentary pang of guilt again. The odds were hugely against Stan, and her team of 1st's might not fare much better in the long run. Her own time would come soon enough though …but even that thought came with a wave of concern for Zenna. As well as her mind, she might also be sharing her fate!

Zenna picked up on it. 'I'm you, remember? Your fate is my fate, my fate is your fate. I get it. It's not like we don't know why we're here, Evelyn Marcin.'

They looped their stoic resolve back and forth between them until it amplified to a level that made their heads buzz …they were ready.

. . .

They arrived at the high mezz without further incident, which just added to the eeriness. The Core was locked down, so it was no surprise to find it deserted. The *EYE* was surely aware of their presence though and would have local resources at her disposal …but still, the area around the consulate was completely silent. Evelyn felt the ghost of when she had been there before – that first speech by a much younger, headstrong and more innocent Evelyn Marcin to a hopeful but frightened crowd. She'd told them that they were at the start of something, that *they* were the start of something. Who could have guessed where it would lead? Who could have foreseen the knife-edge they balanced on?

Zenna followed, mind already as silent and empty as the mezz itself in preparation to be an extension of Evelyn's will ...ironically in a way, not unlike the crowd on that first day.

They stood side by side facing the tall entryway of the consulate of the *EYE*. Zenna took a hold of her hand as a child might... as another child once had – Evelyn was again reminded of her hazy infant memory (or dream?) She had no way of knowing which, but it felt real. For some reason she hoped it was. The doors slid open as she had expected they would.

Hello, old friend.

Chapter Twenty-One

Gaudynya looked serene in an unconscious state that was more than sleep. She lay on the platform like a sorceress on a black altar. She'd even dressed for the part in a midnight blue full-length gown, and an actual real silver tiara. Her hair was loosely tied and rested on her right shoulder. There was no sign of any restraint or medical attachments. Next to her was an identical platform. After the lack of resistance on their journey in, Evelyn had expected there would be ...this was the one party the *EYE needed* her to be at. The second platform probably hadn't been in place when Gaudynya had arrived, and she likely had no awareness of it.

Did she not wonder at all why hers wasn't in the centre of the room?

Evelyn was pretty sure it was something she would have noticed herself.

When she was in position, they would be head-to-head, figuratively and literally. Her blood ran cold at the thought. This was it... one way in, perhaps no way out... and no choice. Gaudynya was physically vulnerable, and it was a tempting thought to take advantage of the fact, but Evelyn Marcin hadn't travelled two realities eight centuries apart to commit cowardly murder. There was no point coming back to leave things in the same state or worse than if she had never bothered.

No. This was her one opportunity. Her all or nothing test of faith. The potential gain was a victory for humanity – a fresh start, a new hope, a limitless future – and if she failed... if she failed, they'd all already failed, one way or another.

'One way in, and no choice,' she whispered.

She stood by Gaudynya's side for a moment and looked into her face. It was easy to imagine her upbringing in this world – the selection, the training, the currents of fate that swept her along ...as they had with her. She delicately brushed a fallen lock of hair back into place. She felt sympathy for her. She *empathised* with her. They were almost the same.

'Whatever happens in there Gaudynya, it isn't personal, not for me. I don't know if either of us had much of a chance, or a choice. If I don't make it back, I've forgiven you already.'

With the world outside still sliding toward oblivion she sat on her platform savouring a last deep breath before pulling her legs up and laying herself flat. She sensed that Zenna was ready too, on the other side of the door in the hallway. She closed her eyes and waited... until her body had faded away.

. . .

…She was led at a frantic pace and struggled to keep up. The construct felt limitless – incredibly rigidly ordered but somehow transparent too. Things that were closer were clearer, but it seemed she could slide between layers to anywhere and anything. Right now though, she was following… following a face. Something about it made her realise it wasn't a real face – of course it wasn't – for a start it wasn't connected to a body, or a head. It was a symbol, an icon for the consciousness of the *EYE*.

After a while it stopped. Waiting.

What are you waiting for? Where are we? What do you want me to do?

There were no words and no conventional language she could recognise. The way so far had been highlighted and revealed subtly, but now the *EYE* had reached its limit. The structure ahead faded into a haze of undisciplined broken light. Compared to what she had travelled through so far it was like a multi-dimensional living sculpture of an oceanic oil spill in the medium of light. It was Gaudynya, Evelyn just knew. Not just her though, there was still some artificial form and containment. She was within the construct of the *EYE,* even though it was distinct and separate …*the apex?*

The face was patiently waiting. Evelyn searched for an emotional connection. It was fluid and (almost) organic, not a simple photic image. It's eyes blinked, looked in the direction of haze, and then looked back to her. There *was* something – not exactly human emotion, not anywhere near rich or deep enough – but it wasn't *not emotion* either. It was an analogue created from something that emotion wasn't made of. It was artificial and alien – but in its own way it was real, and it *was* there. She found it comforting in its simplicity. Human emotion was anything but. People were a constantly shifting mix of duplicitous elements. Whatever it the *EYE* used, and however it translated, she could believe in its honesty. Somehow, she knew it was on her side …and grateful.

She focused on the veils edge.

How do I do this? Do I just move forward?

The *EYE's* eyes dipped slightly, resembling a nod.

How will I find her?

The eyes closed gently.

Will she find me?

Again, the eyes dipped in the manner she took to be a nod.

I guess this is it then. Goodbye old friend. It would be nice to see you again …after.

The face smiled. It wasn't quite right, but as before, she found comfort in its unpolluted, un-duplicitous, unhuman honesty…

. . .

…The group of children already in the room all knew one another. It didn't matter though, as all were intimidating enough individually. They seemed older – was that why they appeared so much more organised and self-assured, and stronger? Her physical size suddenly felt like an issue …the biggest issue! How could she hold her own against kids who would be larger and stronger than her even if she were the same age?

A corrosive whisper was entwined with the imagery… *Weaker… Smaller… Inexperienced… Inadequate…*

The scene somehow became a woman in childbirth… but there was a sinister presence here too…

waiting... waiting to take the child! ...and that awful whisper still tightening around her throat and chest...

How can someone who has no mother believe she can be a mother?

...mocking laughter...

How could she believe she could protect an infant here?

... cold hilarity...

...selfish. Who would be so irresponsible, and so cruel to a defenceless child?

Then she was in water – the lake! She was under the water! Even here there was that chilling whisper... *out of your depth... drowning... drown!*

Her strength and will had gone, completely replaced by fears and insecurities. What did she need to remember? Something about a tether? Something about...?

Tendrils of the insidious whisper followed her down though... *drowning... you know what that feels like don't you, Evelyn Marcin? Running out of road? Running out of air? Running out of life? Reaching for something unreachable... the surface... the moon hanging above you in the black sky...*

She was sure a different whisper had helped to finish that last sentence though. Something warmer perhaps? *...the moon hanging above you in the (black) sky...*

Even though she was being crushed by infinite cold, she was burning... burning in a cold black fire. She didn't know if her lungs would explode or implode, but whatever, she just wished it would be quick.

You need to get out of the water, or you will DIE here! Your CHILD will DIE here!! Go back the way you came. You're DYING, Evelyn Marcin! You're DROWNING!!! Your daughter is DROWNING!!!!

She flailed wildly, trying to go back the way she came, trying to get out of the freezing black water... or fire... or whatever it was that could freeze and crush and burn you all at the same time as pulling you apart from the inside...

The friendly whisper came again. It was warmer. It bravely stayed with her too. She could still feel her life fading though. Perhaps it was an angel, come to take her home...

(Evelyn Marcin... the moon hanging above you in the sky... remember... what happened next?)

Suddenly she had something to hold onto in the swirling black maelstrom. Something she recognized. Something untouchable and immune. A warm hand wrapped around her own.

And the insidious whisper seemed to panic... *No!!! ...there is no warmth, not for you. No hand to help you. Who would care? You don't even care yourself. It isn't real. It's just an illu...*

Illusion?

No!!! Desperate false hope of a dying mind. Go back!!!

An Illusion?

NO! you're DYING!!!

The friendly whisper smiled now with a pure love that started to light and warm the crushing black water. The fear subsided, not gradually, but rapidly. It fell away like meltwater off a spring mountain. The cold, the pressure, the fire, the blackness, the questioning of will... all were things she knew well enough for real, and this wasn't! She found herself staring down each sensation like it was a picture in a book, an illusion. She had something behind her now – that warm and friendly ghost, helping her like wind in a sail… Zenna!

No. Get out, Marcin!

Who's afraid now, Gaudynya? I've been there and got the souvenir for everything you can throw at me. Look at my pain if you like. Look at my fear if you dare. Use everything I've ever seen or felt against me. I don't care. I have nothing to hide. I didn't just survive it, I smashed it. Nothing beat me… and neither will you…. *failure.*

You won't find any failings here, Marcin.

Anyone can say the words Gaudynya, it doesn't mean you believe them. The only thing I'm likely to drown in here is your self-doubt. It pours out in torrents. Why don't we take a look at your failure? Let me see it…

The insidious presence that had been squeezing her loosened its grip. There *were* fears.

Keep your dirty, stilted, orphan, loner loser pathetic-ness to yourself.

You're right, Gaudynya, I'm all of that, and perhaps not much more …and I'm still loved anyway.

Something of Gaudynya's essence recoiled at that.

Is that your thing Gaudynya, love? Was that the making of a failure?

No one loves you, Marcin. People love me… Verrana… Saska would die for me. Defensive, and then angry. *You claim to be loved because an emotionally vacant lump sticks to the only thing that is as damaged and deficient as he is. And even at that, he still loves another.*

It hurt. But she didn't allow herself to be driven back. Instead she focused her awareness to the pain and fear. She knew what it was, and she knew she could defeat it.

The first woman who pays him any attention. A real woman. Strong, intelligent, powerful. A woman with a future at least.

Stan has an open heart. He can't be any other way. You know as well as I do Gaudynya, what he feels for her is nothing like what he feels for me.

Tell yourself, Marcin. Weak... Unpopular... Burden... Loner...

Evelyn struck back at Gaudynya's Achilles though, her fear of failure and lack of attachment.

You know, all the power in the universe will never bring you any fulfilment. Life is nothing without love.

Gaudynya presented stock images of Verrana and Saska. *Getting pregnant isn't love, you fool.*

Who's the fool, Gaudynya. You can't see the difference between what you're showing me and what I'm trying to show you. It doesn't matter who loves me or who loves you. What *I* feel is from me. It's real ...and it's unconditional.

More imagery arose in their shared pit of consciousness, images of the dead now. Images of the burned lifeless husks of people Evelyn had known from the earliest days of the outside settlement. Gaudynya was caught between finding something powerful enough to counteract them, and just trying to block them with emptiness. It was futile. They weren't just images Evelyn had stolen, images from Gaudynya's own memory. They were much more now – multidimensional renderings, each with a past, each connected to all of the others through hopes, fears, loves, and family. All infinite wells of memory and potential, woven in an infinity of other wells of memory and potential... or at least they had been before they were murdered. Murdered by Gaudynya.

Is this how your love manifests, Gaudynya? Is this how you value yourself above all others? Is this the price we will all pay for an eternity of your brand of 'love'? Can you compare our shame now? Because if you don't see it here, you don't even recognise it. You don't have the capacity for it.

Gaudynya's signature began to retreat from the onslaught of every real emotion, tagged, if only by proxy, to every real soul that no longer existed because of her.

Show... me... *my*... shame, Gaudynya.

Flashing images of the fear and drowning and flaming lungs flailed desperately in Gaudynya's confusion. She found the bullet hole in Krasken's lolling lifeless head, and somehow couldn't even weigh that against the... *love*.

Calmly and compassionately Evelyn replaced each attack with her memory of Stan's hand as it had first wrapped around her own at the lake. It was warm in ways Gaudynya had never experienced. It had lifted her from the freezing black hell without effort or assistance. It asked nothing in return as she rose from the darkness.

Then his eyes appeared as she had seen them for the first time, when her own were eventually able to focus again. They said everything when both their voices failed.

If all you have is anger, fear, hate and envy... you have nothing at all, Gaudynya.

Everything I showed you was your own, pulled from your own mind.

The only parts you can see. For me they are the smaller part, and a part I can live with.

Gaudynya was shrinking and retreating. She couldn't escape her own collapsing will.

You can't be this strong. You're not this strong, Marcin. The whispers were mumblings of a breaking heart though.

Invulnerable versus vulnerable. Independent versus dependent. Which is more powerful, Gaudynya? In both cases, only one is truth, the other illusion. Do I need air to breathe? ...yes. Do I need sustenance for my body? ...yes. Do I need love? ...yes. Do I need help? ...yes. I embrace my vulnerability, and I embrace my dependence... and that's what makes me stronger, Gaudynya.

Images of her dead friends, Gaudynya's victims, pressed in again, with compassion this time.

Stay if you like, Gaudynya. Stay and rule the universe at my side... and I will show you love every single second of every single day. Stay, and learn what it is to be a human being and know that you can never actually be one.

Gaudynya retreated into her basest self. She was closed, silent, mind curled in on itself like an embryo.

Now that you no longer believe in your invulnerability, you will learn to love, because I will never abandon you ...and I am infinite.

Chapter Twenty-Two

Zenna came to, slumped against the entryway of the chamber where she had helped Evelyn Marcin neutralise one of most dangerous threats humanity had ever faced – Gaudynya. A single human being, but one who had somehow managed to embody every negative and dangerous trait that had ever blighted history. An individual whose artificial enhancements and opportunities had created a perfect storm capable of bringing a billion years of evolution to a dramatic conclusion.

...and yet in the end, she was just as fragile and vulnerable as any other after all.

From further down the hallway came the sounds of desperate voices and heavy running feet. Whoever they were, whichever side they believed they were on, they would be with her in seconds. She was recovering quickly, but still too drained to move. What did she need to do now anyway? What needed to be done had been done.

She could hardly have looked less threatening as they approached with weapons raised. A middle-aged man who was obviously not from any division of *SecCore* or anyone's equivalent made his way to the front. Anxiety and urgency were carved on his face. His voice managed to stay calm though, almost soothing.

'Do you know where she is? Is Evelyn in there?'

She thought about stalling and playing dumb. Scenarios of how that might work ran abstractly through her mind. It felt like she had just woken still half in a dream.

'Listen,' he said reassuringly. 'We're her friends. We're here to help. Try to focus. You're not in any trouble, and neither is she.'

Another man's voice interrupted harshly from behind him. He was larger and younger, with spiky blonde hair. He seemed familiar even though they had never met.

'No easy way to get in there, Jeremy. One entry, one exit, and this is it. We'd have to cut through or use explosives. Neither is an option. One takes too long, the other's too dangerous.'

Even his character was familiar. Desperation couldn't camouflage who he was. A part of him was a part of her, so much so that she had recognised it instantly.

'You need to prepare yourself, Stan' she told him, still sounding weak. 'She's alive but...'

Stan was almost desperate enough to shake her now. 'How do you know who I am? Who are you?'

Jeremy touched his shoulder. 'Stan, she's a reader. Just need give her a second.'

Stan glared angrily but allowed himself to be guided back a step to give her space.

Jeremy patiently tried again with her. 'I don't want to rush you, but she probably needs our help in there. If we can't stop what is happening...'

Zenna, still dreamy and dazed, suddenly looked at him with surprise. 'You know too, don't you?'

Jeremy looked confused for a second, and then it changed to awkwardness. 'Try and be calm. Just focus. What is your name?'

Zenna nodded wearily. The secret Evelyn carried was one she didn't even know herself, and one that needed to stay secret. She was horrified at how close she'd just come to revealing it even existed.

'Yes... my name... Zenna.' She was looking at Stan again. 'Things are going to be different now.'

Stan breathed deep, trying to be patient. 'Zenna, if we don't get to her soon, things are going to be none-existent. Just tell us if you know a way in. Is she even in there? Do you know anything that can help us?'

She was so drowsy. She couldn't think quite what to say.

He turned his back on her in frustration. 'The bloody world's about to end and the girls taking a nap.'

Etta had stayed out of it so far, unwilling to come between Stan and his beloved Evelyn. She had to consider things he couldn't though. 'Stan, if this is it, if this is where they access this *Apex* or whatever the hell it is, we need to get in there... now. We can rig something to blast through it. There's no choice, and she would understand that. We can't risk Gaudynya getting to it first.'

He shook his head, resigned. 'I know, Etta.'

. . .

Jonas was conflicted on levels he didn't know he could be. Before all this he believed independence from Earth would be unthinkable for another two centuries ...and then he'd been *forced* to think about it, and he'd pretty much come to terms with it. He had empathy for the people who were effectively held as prisoners in Earth's cities, and he'd come to terms with the fact that his actions would also bring harm to them. He had also resolved to see through the unthinkable, not to waver, not to hesitate… but then Evelyn Marcin had turned up again, entering Neam to dangle a tantalising scrap of hope – hardly anything at all, but impossible to ignore. It had to be ignored though, didn't it? Hadn't they passed the point of no return? Wouldn't hesitation be fatal?

'Commander, have you seen what is happening down there?'

The voice broke in on his solitude. He'd wanted to be alone when the final commands and codes were given for the *Smash*. It was a historical moment, but not one to be celebrated, not one for receiving plaudits and congratulations. It was a time for a clear head and full awareness of the consequences. It was a time for cold judgement.

Annoyed at the interruption he reauthorized the connection to respond. 'What is it?'

'View the *EYE's* primary air defences in SE/1-17.' The voice paused to allow Jonas time to find the relevant satellite feed.

'What you see there is happening everywhere. It's the same picture at every Striker facility on every continent.'

There was moment of silence as Jonas watched and tried to comprehend the scale and meaning of the event.

'…Commander?'

'Stand everything down. I mean absolutely everything. And do it right – we don't want to risk any accidents now.'

'Commander, can you reconfirm that order with the appropriate codes please. I read, stand all offensive systems and operations down. Stand the *Smash* down.'

Jonas switched to visual to complete the order and authorisations.

. . .

He hadn't left his office since giving the order. He was joined again now though by the hollo presence of the Prime Representative, who looked less than pleased. Her larger and brighter than life intrusion in the room would have been intimidating enough without her aura of almost wits-end panic.

'You authorised a full stand down without any consultation, Commander. The fact that the possibility had been overlooked should illustrate to you the insanity of it. Perhaps even more insane is the fact that your command hasn't been relieved yet, or that you haven't been placed in detention. What the hell are you thinking, Jonas?'

It was important to hold his nerve now and state his case intelligently – the lives of Earth's citizens depended on it. Perhaps their own did too in the long run. 'Prime Representative, the *EYE* has disarmed itself completely and unilaterally. The fact that we overlooked *that* scenario is an indication of its significance now. It is a complete and irreversible capitulation. I understand the temptation to strike while she is at her most vulnerable... but surely, she's given us the luxury of time to consider. Please, let us take a breath and think this through. We know the consequences, and six months ago we would have done anything to avoid those consequences. Now we have come to terms with them, it seems we can't wait to usher in an age of chaos. Earth is defenceless. The cities are defenceless. The *EYE* is defenceless… and for the first time in its history. We have the time and a moral duty to re-evaluate.'

The Prime Representative looked like a good night's sleep had eluded her for some time. Her nerves were frayed. Jonas knew she considered the burden to be hers alone, just as he knew he considered it to be *his* alone. He knew what it felt like, and he knew what it could do to a person. Talking her down might be less than straight forward.

'You know her power, Jonas,' she countered desperately. 'You know we are up against the ultimate strategist in the universe. Can we afford to believe that this isn't a diversion? Can we afford to believe she has no other more dangerous weapons at her disposal? If she had, do you think they would be on display?'

He thought about it again. Obviously, he'd considered it already. There was every chance she was right. It was a logical possibility when dealing with a definitively logical entity. She could be right… but his gut told him she wasn't. A commander and a Prime Representative were not expected to be at odds between head and heart though.

'Are you aware of an old story about a turtle and a scorpion?' he asked her.

'Jonas, have you lost your mind?'

'…Their existence, their whole universe is at stake. If they cannot do the one thing that is most fundamentally alien to their nature, they will die. If one of them can, but the other cannot, both will still die. The only thing that can save them, save both of them, is their faith. They must trust one another to survive. If we trust the *EYE,* we may not live to regret it, but if we don't…well, six months ago we thought we knew the answer to that question. I don't believe much has changed. We need it. It needs us.'

'So, you want to go full reverse thrust on the biggest decision we have ever made, because of what... a child's story?' She sounded tired, and more than a little exasperated.

Jonas was still hopeful though. She sounded like she *wanted* to be convinced. It would have to be all heart though; the logic was always going to be shaky.

'I'll tell you who told me that story, Marie, and why.'

He took the liberty of using her name.

'My father. I first heard it as a child of course, but I was reminded of it much later, not long before he passed in fact. Did you know of his connection with her, with Evelyn Marcin?'

Clearly, she had been aware but shook her head looking confused. 'I suppose I was aware at the time. Elleng Ettra was a highly respected First Citizen. I imagine anyone's judgement would be influenced by his position on any given issue. It seems the reasoning behind your decision might be coming into clearer focus now.'

'I'm happy for that to be the case. I never met Marcin personally, but I know that my father had high regard for her... very high regard. So much so that he made a point of discussing her when he was close to passing. He considered her part of his final wishes. Our paths never crossed though, and soon after she landed back on Earth, she disappeared again. I forgot about her, like most did. He related that tale in his final days, specifically in relation to her and the *EYE*. It meant nothing to me at the time, and I'd forgotten about it... until now. My father was an eccentric romantic, everyone knew that. He believed in people though, and more specifically, he believed in her. I think…' He almost couldn't believe he was going to say it… that this was his actual pitch. '…he wanted me to believe in her too.'

The Prime Representative tried to smile compassionately at him through her fixed frown. She'd wanted to be convinced. She'd hoped for some shred of real evidence that could justify the stand down. At least now she knew beyond any doubt that there was none. That this was one of those rare and uncomfortable occasions when a choice would have to be made solely on faith, or lack of it.

'You're asking us to believe that Marcin marched her little self into Neam, and somehow managed to convince the *EYE* that the game was up.' She sighed, 'At least you're not trying to sell it as anything *less* ridiculous. The rest of us don't have the benefit of fatherly endorsement, Jonas. This will have to come from me and be entirely on my shoulders. I advise you to be suitably low-key about the initiation and details of our stand-down… and this conversation. I certainly don't want to hear again about the moral life dilemmas of turtles, or any other fairy stories. Are we clear about that?'

'Very clear, Prime Representative.'

If all he would have to endure for his action was ridicule, it was a price worth paying. The Prime Representative was herself now a co-conspirator of the new heart and gut instinct fellowship anyway. She would soon have to find her own way of creatively selling their position to their peers and colleagues across the seven locations of humanity in the solar system. She had by far more the more difficult part to play, and he didn't envy her.

. . .

Zenna suddenly seemed more lucid, as if the chaos within her mind had been disconnected somehow. Jeremy noticed it in her eyes before she had even had chance to speak.

'Are you alright, Zenna?' he asked.

His question broke in on Stan and Etta's anguish. Their attention turned back to her too. As with Jeremy, they could see something was different now from a moment before.

Etta gave Stan a *let me try* look and spoke to her gently. 'You look better. Do you remember where you are? Do you know *who* you are? What's your name?'

Zenna had become a person they hadn't met yet... confident, competent and coherent. She shook her head dismissively and answered, 'Zenna. The consulate. And you can all calm down and take a breath now. It's over.'

Stan took a sharp intake of breath that might have fuelled a verbal tirade if the very assertive hand of Etta hadn't been raised in front of his face in a *back off* gesture.

She tried again. 'What do you mean, *it's over?* What's over, Zenna?'

Zenna peered around her at Stan. 'No offence, but I probably need to speak to the big guy before he does something stupid or has a stroke. You're Stan. That's not a question... I know you are. I've seen you ok, in here.' She tapped the top of her head. 'This is a difficult concept to grasp, so try and follow please. We had an idea, and not a lot of time to practise, but it worked. Evelyn used my... I don't know what to call it... mental kinetics? to reinforce her own. It's complicated... I try to keep up and copy her pattern to amplify its effect. I see what she sees and feel what she feels. We create a feedback loop. Now that she's in and everything has been stood down, I don't think she needs me anymore, other than to explain it to you.'

Stan was trying to stay calm but still struggled to hide his impatience. 'I'm sure she will be able to explain it herself if things fine. Why don't you just tell me where she is and how to get to her, Zenna?'

'This is what I have to explain. You're not going to be able to *get to her*, not for a while at least. She's immersed in the *Apex*. She's an integral part of the framework of the *EYE*. It takes all of her mental effort, Stan. I don't know how long it will be for… not forever, but not soon I don't think either. This is a crucial time.'

Etta was watching him closely. These were things he needed to hear and question, but she wanted to make sure he was handling it. He looked back trying to guess her thoughts. Did she believe any of it? What should they do about it?

He was still looking as he replied. 'If this *Apex* needs someone, a human mind, we can work on that. Under normal circumstances, Eve would definitely be up for it. These aren't regular circumstances though. She's pregnant.'

Zenna was full of empathy for Stan, but after everything else his pain was unbearably draining. She was also aware of the possibility of being called on again by Eve, and the need to conserve her energy. It felt like cheating, but she was going to have to help him build a framework to accept what he was hearing.

She forged away gently. 'I know. The child will be safe. She will be looked after and delivered at full term.'

A burst of emotion suddenly flared from deep within him and she realised why immediately.

He was almost breathless and had tears in his eyes. '*She?*' he gasped. 'A *girl?*'

'Yes Stan, you're going to have a daughter. Like I said, she will be looked after. There's actually no safer place in this world she could be right now.'

At first, she worried the slip would make things harder. It surprised her that the opposite happened. It made everything real for him... and he trusted her now. Etta, fighting the moisture in her own eyes, put an arm around his shoulder, reinforcing the comfort and trust even more. There was clearly a bond between them. It might have begun as attraction, but it was developing into a deep and trusting friendship. It was a good thing too. Etta would be invaluable in shoring up his resilience in the months ahead.

Zenna addressed both of them now. 'Evelyn has a pivotal destiny. She has a job to do. No one knows better than you two how she will cope with that... but the same goes for the rest of us. She can stabilise things, but she can't force people to come together from inside the *EYE*. The *Infinity Corps* will lead the way in that respect.'

Stan had a question. Zenna knew what it was before it left his lips. The answer would be difficult to hear – but as she knew the question, he already knew the answer.

'Can I... can we speak to her? Can we send and receive messages... for coordination?'

She shook her head and tried not to look sad. 'It isn't like that. I don't know exactly what it *is* like, but it isn't like that. Between us and her is everything that the *EYE* is and has ever been.' She thought about it some more though. 'On the other hand, between the *EYE* and us is effectively Evelyn. She has no voice and no language, but she's in there. In a way, when we speak to the *EYE* we will be speaking to Evelyn, and when the *EYE* speaks to us it will also be *through* Evelyn. Don't get your hopes up for conversation as you know it. Like I said, she has no language or voice of her own.'

Stan rubbed his face. 'Where do we even start?'

Jeremy put a hand on his shoulder. 'We already have.'

And Etta slapped his other. 'She's given us what we've been fighting for ...the right to ask that question.'

Thank you for reading INFINITY SHIFT! If you enjoyed it, why not take time to share your thoughts and leave a review. It really helps the little indie □

You can read about how Evelyn and Stan first met in DOWNTIME SHIFT.

Printed in Great Britain
by Amazon